TAK

12/14

P9-BVM-675

## Please Leave in Book

CA
CH
HE
~~KI~~ Apr/15
LH
LU
M/C
PA
PE
RI
SB
SO
TA
TE
TI
TO
WA
WI

# INSATIABLE APPETITES

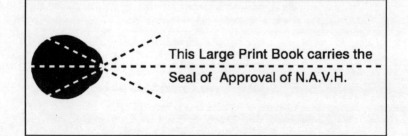

This Large Print Book carries the
Seal of Approval of N.A.V.H.

# INSATIABLE APPETITES

## STUART WOODS

**THORNDIKE PRESS**
*A part of Gale, Cengage Learning*

GALE
CENGAGE Learning·

Farmington Hills, Mich • San Francisco • New York • Waterville, Maine
Meriden, Conn • Mason, Ohio • Chicago

**GALE**
CENGAGE Learning®

**LIBRARY OF CONGRESS CATALOGING-IN-PUBLICATION DATA**

Woods, Stuart.
    Insatiable appetites / Stuart Woods. — Large print edition.
    pages cm. — (A Stone Barrington novel) (Thorndike Press large print basic)
    ISBN 978-1-4104-7500-8 (hardcover) — ISBN 1-4104-7500-X (hardcover)
    1. Barrington, Stone (Fictitious character)—Fiction. 2. Private investigators—Fiction. 3. Large type books. I. Title.
PS3573.O642I57 2015b
813'.54—dc23                                            2014044536

Published in 2015 by arrangement with G. P. Putnam's Sons, a member of Penguin Group (USA) LLC, a Penguin Random House Company

Printed in the United States of America
1 2 3 4 5 6 7 19 18 17 16 15

# INSATIABLE APPETITES

# 1

Election night, late.

Stone Barrington sat on a sofa in the family quarters of the White House, watching the presidential race unfold on television. Things were not going as he had hoped. The race, between Katharine Lee, First Lady of the United States, and Senator Henry Carson of Virginia, seemed to be a dead heat.

Kate Lee and her husband, President Will Lee, were Stone's friends, and he had looked forward to their invitation to spend election night in the family quarters with a couple of dozen good friends. He had not looked forward to seeing her lose the race to a cardboard cutout of a Republican senator, which was how he saw Henry Carson, known in the Lee campaign as Honk, due to a failed attempt to get the nation to think of him as a Hank, instead of a Henry. A mispronunciation by a French official had rechristened him.

Ann Keaton, the Lee deputy campaign manager, to whom Stone was very, very close, came and sat beside him.

"How do you feel about all this?" he asked Ann.

"Nauseous," she replied.

"What's going wrong?"

"We're not getting the turnout our pollsters told us to expect," she said. "Young people and independents are not voting in the numbers we had hoped. At least, that's what our exit polling is telling us. Also, Florida is taking a hell of a long time to count. They've got a Republican governor, and we're worried about hanky-panky. It could be Bush–Gore all over again. On top of that, Ohio is neck and neck."

"The West Coast polls close in ten minutes," Stone said. "Those states should give Kate a boost."

"They should, yes, but California can't put her over the top, if Florida and Ohio go the other way. This could be a very big upset."

"Something's happening," Stone said, pointing at the TV. Chris Matthews and Tom Brokaw were on screen.

"Based on our own exit polling and with eighty-nine percent of the precincts reporting," Brokaw was saying, "our desk is calling Florida for Senator Henry Carson."

"No!!!" came a shout from around the room. "Not possible!" Senator Sam Meriwether of Georgia, Kate's campaign manager, yelled.

"Easy, Sam," Will Lee said. "It's not necessarily over because a network has called it."

"CBS has called it that way, too, but ABC is holding out," a woman watching another TV set called.

"Fox called it for Honk half an hour ago," somebody said.

"I regard that as encouraging," Stone said, and everybody laughed, releasing some tension in the room.

Kate Lee emerged from the Presidential Bedroom with a coat over her shoulders. "I'd better get over to the armory," she said. "I'm going to have to make a statement soon."

"It's not over yet," her husband said.

"I hope you're right," Kate said, kissing him, "but I'd better be ready." She started for the door, two Secret Service agents in tow.

"Wait a minute!" Sam Meriwether shouted. "CBS is reconsidering their call."

9

Kate stopped. "Have they reversed themselves?"

"No, but they're saying that Florida is back in the undecided column."

"That has to be a good sign," Ann said to Stone.

"I hope so."

"New totals from Florida," Sam called out. "With ninety-six percent of precincts reporting, Kate leads by three thousand votes!"

Kate walked back toward the TV set. "That's too narrow a margin. What precincts haven't reported?"

Sam pointed at a north Florida county.

"That county is nearly all African-American," Kate said. "It should be ours by a big margin."

"I'm thinking hanky-panky," Sam said.

"Have we got anybody in the courthouse there?"

As they watched, cars pulled up in the courthouse square and men in suits got out.

"Republicans?" somebody asked.

"FBI agents! I see badges."

The men swept into the courthouse.

Will came and stood beside Kate. "You're right," he said, "you'd better get over to the armory. They've got a comfortable room for you to wait in there. Don't do anything precipitous."

Kate kissed him again and ran for the door.

"The West Coast has closed," somebody called.

"MSNBC is backing away from their call in Florida," somebody else said.

"What do they know that we don't?" Stone asked Ann.

"I don't know anymore," Ann said. "I'm through reading exit polls and guessing. We'll know soon anyway."

"One precinct in north Florida has reported and that, alone, has widened Katharine Lee's lead by another two thousand points," Chris Matthews said. "And we're hearing that they'll have a statewide count at any minute."

"Here's some good news for the Lee campaign," Brokaw said. "Now that the polls in the West have closed, we can tell you that our exit polls show Katharine Lee winning California by nearly thirty points."

A cheer went up around the room.

"We've got a report from Ohio," Brokaw said. "Let's go to Amy Roberts there. Amy?"

"Tom, this is official. All Ohio votes are in, and Kate Lee has won by less than twenty thousand votes!"

There was a roar of glee from the people

present. Will Lee was on his cell phone, and everybody knew who he was calling.

Five minutes later, Florida came in with a final vote. "Katharine Lee has won Florida by thirty-one thousand votes!" Chris Matthew said. "We can now call the election. The next president of the United States will be Katharine Lee!"

"Will," Stone called, "did you reach Kate?"

"Yes, and she's hearing that Henry Carson is about to speak."

Carson came on camera before a big crowd and waved for silence. "Well," he said, "we haven't heard from Guam, yet." His crowd both laughed and moaned. "But it's clear that our next president will be Kate Lee. I congratulate her for the campaign she ran and the victory she has won. I will do all I can to help her."

The TV switched now to the armory, where Kate was making her way to the podium. Will was not with her by design; he had wanted her to accept or concede on her own terms. She stood for nearly ten minutes, waving at the crowd and waiting for the noise to die down. Eventually, the floor was hers.

"Thank you all," she said, "and my thanks to every American who voted today, no matter for whom. Once again, we are on the brink of new leadership in our country, just the way the framers of the Constitution wanted it. I promise you the best government I can put together, and I invite our Republican friends to help us make this country better than ever!" Finally, when she could speak again, she said, "Will, I know you're watching. Unpack!"

Back at the family quarters, people were pounding Will Lee on the back and opening more champagne.

Stone sank into the sofa, relieved and grateful, happy to be in this room on this night.

# 2

Stone felt Ann ease from his bed, then heard her get into a robe and slip from the Lincoln Bedroom. He looked at the clock. Half past five.

Wide awake now, he got out of bed and into some trousers and a shirt, then left the room, looking for coffee, following the scent. He walked into the big oval room and found a table of pastries and a coffee urn. He drew himself a mugful and turned to find a seat.

"Good morning," a female voice said.

Stone turned to find Kate Lee sunk into an armchair, coffee in her hand. "Good morning, Madame President-Elect," he said. "May I be the ten thousandth to congratulate you?" He took a chair facing hers.

"I couldn't sleep," she said. "Will is out like a light, but my mind is still racing."

"I'm not surprised."

14

"For years I couldn't let myself believe this could happen, and now it has, and I still can't believe it."

"Enjoy your disbelief," he said. "It will get real soon enough."

She checked her watch. "Right now, it's just another early morning at home. In a couple of hours all hell will break loose. I must remember to find time to write in my journal today." She patted her belly. "He/she will want to read that someday."

"You still don't know?"

"I know I'm out of fashion, but I don't want to know until I can hold him/her in my arms. Neither does Will."

"Maybe this is callously political of me," he said, "but I think your being pregnant is going to be a material advantage to your presidency."

"I hadn't allowed myself to think of that," Kate replied. "How an advantage?"

"It's going to be hard for your opponents to criticize a pregnant woman," Stone said. "I've noticed that men are very delicate with women who are carrying a child."

"That's true in its way."

"I think you should try to get as much as possible accomplished before you give birth."

"After that, I'll just be another mom, huh?"

"Men aren't afraid to argue with their moms."

Kate laughed. "God knows I wasn't afraid to argue with mine. What about you?"

"I learned early on that my mother had an annoying tendency to be right. It was daunting, and I thought twice before I opposed her."

"You were a smart boy."

"That's what she used to tell me."

"Stone, I want to appoint you to something."

He held up a hand. "No, please, Kate."

"Shut up. This is your president-elect speaking. You are now, officially, the first member of my Kitchen Cabinet."

Stone laughed. "How could I not accept that post? I'm honored beyond words."

"And you will serve for the entire eight years."

"That's thinking ahead."

"A president can get things done in a first term, but she needs a second to keep her opponents from dismantling her accomplishments."

"You've got a narrow majority in both houses — that should help."

"The next congressional campaign starts

16

today," she said, "and so does my charm offensive with Republican congresspeople and senators. They may vote against me a lot of the time, but I'm going to make their hearts break when they do."

"I believe you."

"I heard Ann sneak back to her room a few minutes ago."

"Oops."

"I'm happy that you two were able to get together for a while, and, believe me, I'm sorry that I'm going to be keeping you apart for a long time."

"Thank you. We've talked about that, and we know it has to be done."

"What is it the mafiosi say? This is the business we've chosen."

"Ann knows that."

"I'm glad she does." Kate got to her feet. "I hope you'll be around for a few days."

"No, I have to get back. I've been away from my desk for too long, what with the Paris trip, and I flew a borrowed airplane down here that has to be returned."

"I hear you bought a house in Paris."

"I did, and I have to be careful about doing that every time I get a little depressed. If you and Will ever need a hideaway, it will be waiting for you."

"That's sweet of you," Kate said, patting

his cheek, "but the only hideaway we're going to have is the one we have now at Camp David. And that's sort of like a White House in the woods. We'll take you up on your Paris house when they kick us out of town." She kissed him on the forehead and padded out of the room.

Stone thought maybe he should start a journal of his own.

# 3

Stone said his goodbyes to Ann over a second cup of coffee and was back in his home office in New York in time for a sandwich at his desk, while he went through mail and phone messages. Joan stuck her head in. "Herbie Fisher wants to come by after lunch to catch up."

"Sure. He's been keeping an eye on my clients."

"You're starting to get phone calls from people that sound like they want your ear, because you know our new president."

Stone sighed. "I suppose that's inevitable."

"Especially when your name is on the Lees' guest list for the White House on election night. Did you really sleep in the Lincoln Bedroom?"

"I did, and quite well."

"What's it like?"

"Very Victorian. Lincoln never slept there, but he used it as an office."

"Any ghosts?"

"I was sleeping too soundly to notice."

"How's our Kate looking?"

"Just great. Didn't you watch her on TV?"

"Sure, I did." The phone rang and she went to answer it.

Stone found four letters in his mail that alluded to his friendship with the Lees, and he dictated perfunctory replies.

Herbert Fisher turned up at two o'clock, with a catalog case full of files to return. He accepted a cup of coffee and settled into the sofa.

"Thanks for riding herd on my clients while I was gone, Herb," Stone said.

"Don't mention it. Just vote for my partnership tomorrow."

"Is it tomorrow? I've lost track. You shouldn't have anything to worry about, you know. You've brought more business into the firm than a lot of the partners."

"I still feel a chill here and there."

"That's envy, not doubt."

"I hope you're right."

"You'll be the youngest partner."

"That's what I hear."

"And you've set a record for going from new associate to senior associate to partnership."

"I hear that, too. I think it was too fast for

some of the partners."

"Has Bill Eggers offered you a better office?"

"I'm happy where I am. I did ask for another associate and another secretary, though."

"If the workload demands it, he's not going to turn you down."

"Do you think you'll get new business because of your relationship with Kate Lee?"

"I never got any because of my relationship with Will, and I'd decline anything I thought was nakedly political — or refer it to you."

"Referrals are appreciated."

"Herb, you seem a little down at a time when you should be elated."

Herbie shrugged. "I'm just not sure how I'll like being a big boy in the firm. Being the kid was fun."

"You'll like it at bonus time."

"I already like it at bonus time."

"Bonuses get bigger when you're a partner."

"I guess."

"Herb, is there anything wrong? Anything I can help with?"

He was about to answer when Joan buzzed Stone.

"Yes?"

"Eduardo Bianchi on one."

Bianchi was a kind of mentor to Stone. He knew everybody in town, served on the most prestigious boards, and had his fingers in many pies. He had also been long rumored to have been a power in the mob as a young man and an adviser to it in his maturity, but nobody had ever proved anything.

Stone picked up the phone. "Eduardo, how are you?"

"Better than I have any right to be, Stone." Bianchi was well into his eighties. "Will you come to lunch tomorrow?"

"I'd love to." He had an idea. "May I bring a friend? A young attorney?"

"Of course. I'm always happy to meet your friends. Twelve-thirty?"

"See you then." He hung up. "Herb, I have a lunch invitation for you tomorrow."

"Sorry, I've got a date — new business prospect."

"Reschedule," Stone said.

"Who's lunch with?"

"Eduardo Bianchi."

"I'll reschedule."

# 4

Stone walked up to the Seagram Building the following morning and took the elevator to the highest of the four floors occupied by the law firm of Woodman & Weld. The firm's grandest conference room had rows of folding chairs set up, and all the partners filled the room.

Bill Eggers, the managing partner and Stone's friend from law school, strode into the room, sat down at the head of the conference table, and rapped sharply with his gavel. "The partnership meeting will come to order."

Everyone took their seats and became silent.

"There is only one item on the agenda this morning: the consideration of Herbert Fisher for full partnership. I know that some of you think that Herb has moved a little too quickly through our ranks, but you have only to consider his ability as a rainmaker.

From the first week of his association with us, he has been bringing this firm business, and the importance of his clients to the firm has grown with each year he has spent with us as an associate and senior associate. I have a cashier's check in my pocket for a million dollars, covering his buy-in. Do I hear a motion?"

Stone, a little way down the table, stood. "I am pleased and honored to propose Herbert Fisher for full partnership."

"Do I hear a second?"

There were several shouts of "Second!"

"Without objection," Eggers said, looking around the room with a beady eye, "the motion is carried unanimously." He rapped his gavel again and stood up. "This meeting is adjourned!" He walked quickly from the room, and the partners dispersed.

Stone walked downstairs a flight and found Herbie sitting in his office, reading a contract. He looked up and smiled at Stone. "Something I can do for you, Stone?"

Stone took his hand, pulled him to his feet, and hugged him. "May I be the first to congratulate you on becoming a full partner in Woodman & Weld?"

"You certainly may," Herbie replied.

"Then let's get downstairs. Fred is waiting to drive us to Eduardo's."

Fred piloted the Bentley out to the nether regions of Brooklyn, where Eduardo Bianchi's sixty-year-old Palladian mansion overlooked a fine beach and the sea. They were met at the door by Pietro, Eduardo's longtime factotum and, allegedly, in his youth, assassin, said to be particularly good with the knife. Pietro looked Herbie up and down. Before he could start frisking the younger man, Stone said, "He's with me, Pietro."

The little man led them through the house and into Eduardo's library, where a table had been set for them. At a more benign time of year they would have lunched on the back lawn, near the large, black-bottom pool that had been designed and crafted to look like a lake. Stone introduced the younger man to the elder.

Eduardo looked closely into Herbie's face and held on to his hand for an unusually long time. "I have heard good things said of you," the old man said.

"Stone is too kind, sir."

"Not only from Stone." He let go of Herbie's hand and showed them to their seats.

"Eduardo," Stone said, "Herb was, an hour ago, elected to partnership in Woodman & Weld."

"My hearty congratulations, young man,"

Eduardo said, pressing his hand again.

"Thank you, sir," Herbie replied.

"How are you keeping busy these days, Eduardo?" Stone asked.

"Business," Eduardo replied. "The usual. They won't leave an old man alone."

"I think you would be very unhappy if they did," Stone said, causing Eduardo to emit a rare laugh.

"Perhaps you are right, Stone — you so often are. I hear that is why Katharine Lee thinks so highly of you."

"Do you indeed? Do you know her?"

"Since she was an anonymous CIA analyst," Eduardo said. "I was able to be helpful to her behind the scenes when she was being considered for the directorship, though I don't think she would like that to be public knowledge, now that she will be president."

"I should think she would be proud to have people know that you are her friend."

"She is discreet, and that is better than being proud. It is good, though, that you and I may see more of each other when exercising our duties in her Kitchen Cabinet."

That startled Stone, but only for a moment. Eduardo had a tendency to know things before they became public. "I will look forward to that," Stone said.

Pietro brought antipasti that was passed around, and a crisp white wine, perfectly chilled, was served with it.

"I've never served on a Kitchen Cabinet," Stone said. "What may I expect?"

"I was privileged to serve two other presidents in that capacity," Eduardo said. "First, Lyndon Johnson, though we talked only of domestic matters. I wholeheartedly disagreed with him about Vietnam, and as that wore on we spoke less and less. And then there was Richard Nixon."

Stone blinked, speechless.

"We only rarely talked directly, usually it was through John Ehrlichman, of whom I thought highly. After that little burglary, I withdrew. Dick was so obviously headed for ruin, and none of them would listen to reason."

"Each time we meet I learn something new about you, Eduardo. You should write a memoir."

Eduardo laughed again. "If word got out that I were even contemplating such a thing, not even Pietro would be able to protect me from those who would want my head in a basket. I know far more about too many people than is good for me. Or for them."

"Have you ever written anything, Eduardo?"

"Well, I dabble with my journal from time to time," the old man said. "I'd let you read it, but it is written in a Sicilian dialect that is quite impenetrable to the uninitiated. Sometimes I entertain myself by reading a few pages. There are eight volumes, so far, covering as many decades. They are covered in fine leather — red, the color of the devil!" He laughed and slapped Stone on a shoulder, a remarkably rare display of camaraderie. "When I and all I love are dead, you may publish it, Stone — if you can find a translator!"

"Have you met with Kate yet, Eduardo?" Stone asked.

"Not for a couple of years, but I expect to see her when she comes to New York again during the transition." Eduardo looked thoughtful for a moment. "This Kitchen Cabinet thing could cause you problems, Stone."

"How so?"

"Once you are identified as a member of that group, there are people who might try to damage Kate by damaging you."

"I've already had a whiff of that during the campaign," Stone said.

"All the more reason for them to try again," Eduardo said.

# 5

After lunch, Eduardo gave them a little tour of the house, clearly for Herbie's benefit, showing them his collections of books, sculpture, and pictures.

"I've always loved the Modigliani portrait," Stone said, nodding toward the woman on the wall.

"She is my favorite," Eduardo replied.

"I love the two Picassos," Herbie said, nodding at two paintings hung side by side.

"One of them is a Braque," Eduardo said, looking amused. "See if you can tell me which one."

"The one on the right," Herbie said without hesitation.

"You have quite an eye, Herbert."

"No, I just made a lucky guess."

Everyone laughed.

Stone was amazed at how well the two men got on together. He could remember when Herbie was little more than an overgrown street urchin, chiseling his way through life.

Finally, Eduardo walked them to the front door to say their goodbyes. Pietro approached them and handed Eduardo a very fine alligator briefcase; Eduardo handed it to Stone. "A little gift," he said.

"Thank you, Eduardo." The briefcase was not empty. Stone laid it on the front passenger seat of the Bentley, then Fred drove them away.

"What did Eduardo give you?" Herbie asked.

"I don't know," Stone said. "Maybe a picture. He's given me things like that before."

Fred dropped Stone at home, then drove Herbie back to his office.

Stone set the briefcase on his desk and looked through his messages, then Joan came in.

"Did Herbie make partner?"

"He did," Stone said. "I took him to lunch with Eduardo. They got on amazingly well."

"Nice briefcase," Joan said.

"A gift from Eduardo."

She went back to her desk, and Stone opened the briefcase. Inside were eight slim volumes bound in red leather. The color of the devil, he reflected. He picked up one and opened it. The hand was florid, almost artistic, obviously the product of the teaching of one or more long-gone nuns, but it was incomprehensible to Stone — perhaps even to most Italians.

An envelope was tucked into the volume, and Stone's name was written on it in the same hand. He opened it and read the short note.

*I want these to be in your keeping, Stone. When I am gone there are those who will want them, so be careful.*

Under Eduardo's signature there were four groups of two-digit numbers, but no explanation of them. He read them several times, trying to make sense of them, but nothing came to him.

He took the eight volumes to the big safe in an alcove off his office, opened it, and made room for them on the bottom shelf. One day, he thought, he would try to have them deciphered. He sat down and went to work.

Near the end of the day Joan buzzed him. "Mary Ann Bacchetti is on line one. She says it's important."

Mary Ann was Dino's ex-wife, the mother of his son, Ben, and Eduardo's elder daughter. Stone picked up the phone. "Hello, Mary Ann." He hadn't spoken to her since

32

Dino's divorce, except in passing.

"Daddy's had a stroke," she said. "He's not expected to live."

Stone was stunned. "I had lunch with him today, and he seemed in great form."

"He's ninety-four," she said. "Nobody that age is in great form. Pietro said that after you and your friend left, he went into his study and dictated some things to his secretary, worked all afternoon. He signed some documents she had typed up, then he complained of a headache and collapsed onto his desk."

"I'm so sorry. Is there anything I can do for you, Mary Ann?"

"It looks as though I'm going to need a better lawyer than I've got," she said. "I'd like to hire you, Stone, and whoever you need from Woodman & Weld."

"Let's not get ahead of ourselves."

"Stone, his doctor thinks he won't make it through the night, and when he goes, all hell is going to break loose, and everything will fall into my lap. It's not too soon to start thinking about that."

"Where did they take him?"

"To his bed. There didn't seem to be any point in taking him to a hospital when his room is well stocked with medical equipment. He hates hospitals and always wanted to be treated at home when he got sick."

"All right, let's meet, then."

"Can you come out here tomorrow morning?"

"Of course."

"Around ten."

"All right."

"And will you call Dino and tell him? I can't deal with him right now."

"All right, but you should call Ben, if you haven't already. He'll want to be here."

"He's already on his way," she said. "And, Stone, not a word to anybody outside our families. I don't want it known that he's dying."

"I understand. I'll see you tomorrow morning." They hung up.

Joan buzzed him. "Your son is holding on line two."

Stone punched the button. "Peter?"

"Hello, Dad. You've heard about Mr. Bianchi?"

"Ben's mother just called me."

"We're on our way to Santa Monica Airport. The studio's jet is bringing us east. We should land around ten tonight."

"I'll have Fred meet you at Teterboro and bring you and Ben to the city. Is Hattie coming, too?" He knew she would be; he never went anywhere without his girlfriend and collaborator.

"Yes, and Tessa, too." Tessa Tweed was Ben's girlfriend, and she had had featured roles in two of his and Peter's films.

"Your old suite will be ready," Stone said. "I'll see you at breakfast."

"Good, Dad. We're looking forward to seeing you."

"Shall I call Hattie's folks?"

"She's doing that now. I'd like for us all to have dinner tomorrow night if . . . circumstances allow."

"Of course. We'll do it here."

"Thank you, Dad. See you at breakfast." They hung up.

Stone called Dino, who was in a meeting. "Please ask him to call me the moment he's free," he said to the policewoman sergeant who guarded Dino's gate. "It's important. Has his son called?"

"Yes, just a moment ago."

"Good." Stone hung up.

Five minutes later, Dino called.

"Have you talked to Ben?"

"No, I've just been handed his message. I called you first."

"Mary Ann called me a few minutes ago."

"Since when is she speaking to you?"

"Eduardo has had a stroke, a bad one. She says he may not live through the night. Ben

35

and Peter and their girls are flying in late tonight, and I'm having them met."

"Where is Mary Ann?"

"At Eduardo's house. She asked me to call you, so she may not be ready to talk to you."

"I'll send a patrol car and some uniforms out there," Dino said. "Keep the press away."

"No one knows he's ill yet. She asked me to keep it in confidence."

"She won't be able to keep the lid on that one for long."

"I had lunch with Eduardo today," Stone said, "and I took Herbie Fisher out there to meet him. He looked wonderful."

"He always does."

"Mary Ann told me he's ninety-four. I had no idea."

"I didn't know that, either. I thought he was, maybe, in his mid-eighties."

"When you talk to Ben, find out where he's sleeping. He's welcome here, of course, but he may want to go to Mary Ann's or your place, or he may want to go to his grandfather's. I'll have Fred take him to wherever he wants to go."

"Thanks, I'll ask him. You want dinner tonight? Viv's away on business."

"Sure. Patroon?"

"Eight o'clock." Dino hung up.

# 6

Stone got to Patroon first, and Ken Aretsky, the owner, joined him for a moment. "How is Eduardo Bianchi, Stone?" Ken asked. "I know you two are close."

"I had lunch with him today," Stone replied, "and he looked wonderful, in very good form."

"I'm glad to hear it," Ken said. "He comes in once in a great while, and I'm always happy to see him."

Stone wondered why Ken happened to bring that up, but he didn't want to ask.

Dino came in and sat down, and a waiter appeared with Knob Creek for Stone and Johnnie Walker Black for Dino. They chatted briefly, then Ken excused himself to greet another customer.

"Have you heard anything new?" Dino asked.

"Not a word, but Ken just asked after Eduardo's health. I thought for a moment he might have heard something, but he didn't say so. Have you heard from Mary Ann?"

Dino shook his head. "Anna Maria and I don't do business." That was her given name, but she had begun using Mary Ann as a teenager.

"She said something odd on the phone. She said that when Eduardo died, all hell would break loose."

"I've no idea what she meant by that," Dino said. "He's an old man, and nobody's going to be surprised when he dies, are they?"

"That's what I thought, but Mary Ann seems to know something I don't."

"She's probably referring to the disposition of his estate."

"She's certainly thinking about that. She asked me and the firm to represent her in settling his affairs."

"My guess is you're not going to find a huge amount in his estate," Dino said.

"You think Eduardo's been concealing assets?"

"Eduardo is a Sicilian. It's in his nature to conceal everything, especially money. I'll bet when you see his will, you'll find there isn't much in there besides the house and some investments."

"I've always had the impression that Eduardo was immensely wealthy," Stone said.

"Back when we were married, Mary Ann thought so, too. Even before she started her investment firm she was helping him with investments, so she knew things that I didn't."

"What sort of investments?"

"I had the impression he was pretty big in real estate, but I don't know what else. Except for his house, which is lavish, he seemed to live fairly simply. There were some practically invisible servants around the place — in addition to the evil Pietro — and Eduardo's dead wife's younger sister lived there and cooked for him until she died a couple of years ago."

"He owns a lot of art," Stone said. "His study, the living room, and the dining room are filled with his acquisitions."

"So are the upstairs rooms," Dino said. "Did you ever go up there?"

"No."

"Have a look around, if you have the chance."

"I may have the chance tomorrow," Stone said. "I'm meeting Mary Ann out there at ten."

"She's right on it, isn't she? She always

39

had a mind like a steel trap, and hands, too."

"Well, I'd rather have a client who is ready to deal with things than one who doesn't want to know."

"I'll bet you two things," Dino said. "One, she already knows a lot. Two, there are things that she doesn't know, that Eduardo kept to himself."

"It will be interesting finding out."

"Oh, Jesus," Dino said, slapping his forehead. "I just thought of something."

"What?"

"Dolce."

Stone gulped. Dolce was Eduardo's younger daughter. Stone had once had a torrid affair with her, ending in their marriage, in Venice. It had been a civil ceremony, and before the religious one could take place, the following day, Stone had been called back to the States. Dolce had followed him, apparently believing that he had jilted her at the altar, and had begun a series of attempts on his life. She was clearly mad, under a placid surface, and Eduardo had locked her away in his house. She kept escaping, continuing her plots against Stone, and finally her father had packed her off to Sicily, where she had been kept in a convent. Stone had received an envelope from Eduardo containing a page from the book they had signed at the Venice town hall upon their marriage. It was the only legal evidence of their union, and Stone had burned it.

"Oh, shit," he said.

"If Eduardo dies," Dino pointed out — unnecessarily, Stone thought — "what's to keep her in Sicily?"

"I wonder if Eduardo had her legally committed?" Stone mused.

"More likely, he just stuck her in that convent and made a generous donation," Dino replied. "That would be more Sicilian. I'd look into that, if I were you."

"Believe me," Stone said, "I will. Listen, I'm having everybody to dinner at my house tomorrow night."

"What time."

"Six-thirty for drinks."

"Viv will be back. We'll be there."

"I'll have to ask Mary Ann, but I doubt she'll come."

"From your lips to God's ear."

41

# 7

Stone called Herbie Fisher at home after dinner, told him about Eduardo, and asked him to work on the new case. The kids arrived after eleven; Stone greeted them all, sent Ben to Mary Ann's apartment, then went to bed.

The following morning, Stone had Joan print out a representation agreement, which was mostly boilerplate, then Fred drove Stone and Herbie to nether Brooklyn. As they turned into the driveway, they were flagged down by a uniformed policeman. They identified themselves and, after a call to the house, were admitted.

Pietro met them at the door, somehow looking older since yesterday, then he led them to Eduardo's study. Mary Ann sat at her father's desk, rifling drawers and peering under the large piece of furniture.

"Good morning, Mary Ann," Stone said. "How is your father this morning?"

"In a deep coma, thank you." She stared at Herbie. "Who's this?"

"Mary Ann, let me introduce Herbert Fisher, a partner at Woodman & Weld, who will be assisting me in this matter."

"Bring us coffee," she said to Pietro, who vanished.

"What were you doing under the desk?" Stone asked.

"Looking for secret drawers," she replied.

"Before we begin, Mary Ann, let me explain a few things about how we will work."

"All right, go ahead."

Pietro appeared with a silver tray bearing a coffeepot, creamer, cups, and a plate of small pastries.

"Leave us," she said to him. "Go ahead, Stone," she said, when the man had gone.

"First of all," Stone said, "we can represent the estate or we can represent you, personally, but not both. Since you are, presumably, an heir, that would be a conflict of interest. Which will it be?"

Mary Ann thought about that for a moment. "You will represent the estate," she said. "I'll find my own attorney."

"Fine. You must understand that we will, in a sense, be representing the court, and that means we must keep you at arm's length while we do our work."

"All right," she said.

"I want to go off the record here for a moment," Stone said. "What I'm now about to say to you is to be confidential among the three of us."

She looked at Herbie, then back at Stone, and her eyes narrowed. "Yes?"

"Before I begin to look at a will or any other documents, I must tell you that we can deal only with those assets mentioned in Eduardo's will and any others listed in financial statements. Is there a will?"

"Yes, it's in a safe behind the bookcase, there," she said, pointing. "I don't know how to open it."

"Does Pietro?"

"He says no."

"Then I will have steps taken to open it. What I meant by my previous statement is that, if Eduardo undertook during his life to remove cash, property, or other assets from his taxable estate by concealing them in secret accounts or corporations, I cannot know about it. I must be in a position to tell the probate court, honestly, that I am not aware of any assets not listed in my petition to the court. Is that clearly understood?"

Her eyes narrowed, and she said softly, "Yes."

"Something else: you are going to have to become accustomed to the idea of the estate's paying very substantial inheritance taxes. If you obsess over taxes, you will start making mistakes that will pile up and are likely to fall on you. From what little I know of Eduardo's affairs, he is very wealthy and, even after taxes, his heirs will come into large sums of money and/or property. You must be content with what's left."

"I understand."

"Good. Now I must ask you, has anything been removed from the house since Eduardo fell ill?"

"I suppose the maid took out the trash."

"I will need to see any trash bags not yet collected," Stone said. "Has any piece of artwork been removed?"

"Not yet."

"You may not remove anything that belongs to the estate from the house, until the court gives permission."

"I understand."

"Who is Eduardo's secretary, and where is she?"

"Her name is Angelina Bono, and she is upstairs with my father."

"Good. When we're done here, please tell

her I'd like to speak with her."

"When will we be done here?"

"We're almost finished, and we're back on the record. Do you know who Eduardo has appointed as his executor?"

"He told me long ago that I would be his executor, and that the fact was in his will, and he has never said anything to indicate that he changed his mind."

Stone removed a document from his briefcase and handed it to Mary Ann. "This is a representation agreement between Eduardo's executor and Woodman & Weld. Please take your time and read it, particularly with regard to our fees, and if you agree, sign both copies." He handed the papers to her. "If we should subsequently learn that Eduardo appointed a different executor, we must have that person execute the document."

Mary Ann read the entire agreement, then signed it, and returned it to Stone.

"Thank you," Stone said. He signed the documents and returned one to Mary Ann.

There was a sharp rap on the study door.

"Come!" Mary Ann said.

Pietro entered the room, looking agitated. "Anna Maria," he said, "your father is awake."

# 8

Mary Ann hurried around the desk. "Come with me," she said, and Stone and Herbie followed her down the hall and up the stairs. The stairway and the upstairs hall were lined with pictures, which Stone wanted more time to look at, but not now.

At the end of the upstairs hallway, double doors opened to a bedroom that could only be described as baronial in size and decor. Eduardo lay in an electric bed that had been raised enough for them to see his face. He was surrounded by beeping, flashing medical equipment, and a doctor, a nurse, and a priest were at his bedside. Eduardo seemed alert and was smiling.

The priest, whom Stone recognized as the cardinal of New York, said, to nobody in particular, "It's a miracle of God."

An elderly woman sitting in a chair on the other side of the room burst into tears.

Stone approached the foot of the bed.

"Good morning, Eduardo," he said. "It's good to see you looking well."

Eduardo struggled a little to speak but finally said, "I am not well. I will die soon."

"That is in God's hands," the cardinal said.

"You may think so," Eduardo replied. He motioned to Stone to approach, and the others stood back a little to allow him near the old man. He raised a hand and beckoned Stone closer. "Everything is in order," he whispered. "It's all in my safe."

Stone wanted to ask him the combination but thought better of it.

"Papa!" Mary Ann said. "Speak to me, tell me what you want."

"You must ask Stone," Eduardo said, then he closed his eyes and his head fell to one side. Next to the bed, a machine that had been beeping now emitted a steady electronic tone, and wavy lines indicating heartbeat and respiration flattened.

"Save him!" Mary Ann said to the doctor.

"Your father signed a do-not-resuscitate order last year," the man said. "There is nothing more I can do for him."

Mary Ann burst into tears, and the nurse led her to a chair.

Stone left the bedside to those attending Eduardo's remains. He took Pietro, who was weeping quietly, aside. "I'm sorry for your loss, Pietro," he said. "Now you must give me all the keys to Eduardo's study."

Pietro beckoned for Stone to follow and led him into a large dressing room, which could have accommodated the stock of a small men's clothing store. Suits, jackets, trousers, and shirts filled it, in neat rows. Pietro went to the top drawer of a built-in dresser, opened it, and handed Stone a bunch of keys on a ring, then he removed a similar ring from his own pocket and handed those over, too. "That is all the keys to the house," he said. "I will need to lock up tonight."

"Thank you, Pietro," Stone said, and pocketed the keys.

Stone went back into the bedroom, approached Mary Ann, who had stopped weeping and was simply staring into the middle distance. "He was a wonderful man," Stone said. "I'll miss him."

He went to the doctor and said quietly, "I am the attorney for the estate. Please give Ms. Bianchi the death certificate."

He turned toward Mary Ann. "Please excuse us." He beckoned to Herbie to follow and left the room.

Stone got out his iPhone and took photographs of the pictures in the hallway, then he went from room to room, peeking in and photographing still more art. Finally, he led Herbie downstairs to the study and closed the doors behind him.

Herbie sank into a chair. "That was dramatic," he said. "What did Eduardo say to you?"

"He said, 'Everything is in order. It's all in my safe.' "

Stone walked to the bookcase Mary Ann had indicated and found a concealed latch that opened it. A double-doored safe, perhaps five feet wide and eight feet tall, occupied the space behind it.

"You want me to get us a safecracker?" Herbie asked.

Stone thought about that and remembered something. He went to the safe, spun the dial, then started turning it back and forth.

"So you're a safecracker now?" Herbie asked.

Stone tried the safe's wheel, but it did not budge. He spun the dial again, and tried it again, this time turning the dial in the opposite direction. He took hold of the wheel and turned it. "Voilà," he said.

"How the hell did you do that?" Herbie asked.

"Eduardo sent me a note with the combination included. He just neglected to say in which direction to start." He closed the door and relocked it, then closed the bookcase.

"Don't you want to see what's inside?"

"Not yet," Stone replied, returning to the desk. "I'd rather do it when Mary Ann isn't around." He sat down and looked through the items she had been removing from the drawers when he had arrived. There was a checkbook showing a balance of more than $150,000, a desk diary and an address book, a gold pocket watch, a gold cigarette case, and a gold Dunhill lighter.

"I didn't realize Eduardo smoked," Herbie said.

"I think he must have quit a long time ago," Stone replied, "but he didn't throw away these elegant accoutrements. I want you to call the office and ask Bill Eggers's assistant to recommend someone to come in and catalog everything in the house. Have them start first thing tomorrow morning."

Herbie got out his phone and made the call.

The door opened and Mary Ann entered. "I've spoken to the cardinal. There will be a high mass said at St. Patrick's Cathedral a week from today at two PM," she said. "I have other arrangements to make, so I will return to my office in the city and make them there. Please begin your work here."

"Mary Ann," Stone said, "I'm getting everyone together for dinner at my house tonight at seven. We'd be delighted if you would join us."

"I'm not sure Dino and his wife would enjoy that, but I'll come if I can. May we leave it that way?"

"Of course. It will be very casual."

She nodded and left, closing the door behind her.

Herbie closed his phone. "Eggers's guy is on it. He'll have a team here tomorrow. Shall we take a look in the safe?"

"Give Mary Ann a few minutes to clear the house," Stone said, "then we'll open it."

# 9

They heard a car door slam and the sound of the vehicle driving away. Stone went to the bookcase, released the catch, and opened it. He entered the combination, spun the wheel, and opened both doors of the safe.

"Very neat," he said. There were shelves and drawers filled with files and a case containing a watch winder behind a glass door. The watches were slowly rotating. On a shelf at waist height was a row of red envelopes, perhaps a dozen of them. "Get a legal pad and let's start making a list of the contents," he said to Herbie, who complied.

Stone started at the left end and removed an envelope. "Last Will and Testament of Eduardo Bianchi," he read aloud, then he returned the envelope to the shelf. He went through the rest of the envelopes: half a dozen of them contained codicils to the will; the others contained up-to-date financial documents: brokerage account statements, a deed to the house, and a financial statement among them.

"The man had an orderly mind," Herbie said, noting each on his pad.

"It looks to me as though Eduardo was preparing to die," Stone said. He took the last envelope from the shelf. "This is addressed to me," he said. He sat down at Eduardo's desk, broke the red wax seal, and removed some sheets of paper. "There's a letter," Stone said. He read it aloud.

My Dear Stone,

My life is drawing to an end. I can feel it coming, and this letter is to appoint you as the attorney for my estate, at your firm's usual fees, and to appoint you as co-executor with my daughter, Anna Maria. Also attached is a letter to Anna Maria, informing her of my decision. You may call upon other members of your firm or outside companies to assist you in the work. Attached to this letter is a list of the other documents in red envelopes in the safe. The attached financial statement is an accurate list of all my holdings, of every kind. I know you will deal with my estate and my heirs impartially, according to the instructions in

54

my will.

I wish to express to you my gratitude for your friendship over the years. Following your life and career helped make my later life more interesting and entertaining, and I always found your company to be most enjoyable.

With affection,
Eduardo Bianchi

Stone couldn't speak for a moment.

"Shall I ask Pietro to collect the garbage bags?" Herbie asked.

Stone nodded, and Herbie left the room, giving him time to compose himself. Stone took some deep breaths and reflected on the many lunches he had enjoyed with Eduardo, how the man had offered the chapel in his house for Stone's marriage to Arrington, and arranged for the mayor of New York to perform the ceremony, not to mention the reception that followed.

Herbie returned. "There were only three bags of trash. I emptied them all and found nothing of any import."

"Let's continue cataloging the contents of the safe," Stone said.

They worked through the day, stopping only for the sandwiches Pietro thoughtfully brought to the study.

"That's everything in the safe," Stone said, returning the last item to its place.

"Shall we read the will?" Herbie asked.

"I think I will reserve that for dinner tonight," Stone said. "His family will all be there, except for Dolce." He made a mental note to discuss her condition with Mary Ann when he saw her. He took the will and the codicils, put them into his briefcase, and snapped it shut. Pietro appeared as if summoned.

"We're done for the day, Pietro," Stone said, handing him his keys to the house. "I've removed the key to the study, and I'll lock up. Tomorrow morning several people will arrive to catalog everything in the house. Please do whatever you can to make their work easier, and, perhaps give them some lunch. It may take them a week or two. I'll be back tomorrow."

"Of course, Mr. Barrington," Pietro said, then left.

Stone closed the safe and spun the wheel, then picked up his briefcase and locked the side door to the study. He stepped into the hall and locked that door, too. As he turned to leave he stopped; six men in black suits were carrying a coffin down the stairs. He and Herbie followed them outside and waited until they had put the coffin into a hearse and driven away.

Fred had returned for them and drove them back to the city.

Early that evening everyone gathered: Peter and Hattie, Ben and Tessa, Dino and Viv. Fred made drinks for everyone.

"How did it go today?" Dino asked.

"Very well. Eduardo saw it coming — he had put his affairs into perfect order. By the way, I invited Mary Ann to dinner, but I'm not sure she's coming."

"Yeah, well, okay," Dino said. "I'll prepare Viv, just in case."

Then Fred showed in Mary Ann, and it was Stone's job to introduce her to Vivian Bacchetti. That went more smoothly than he could have hoped. They were called to dinner.

After they had dined, Stone put his briefcase on the dining table and opened it. He handed Mary Ann the envelope addressed to her and waited for her to read it. She nodded.

"I thought this might be a good time to read the will," Stone said, "since everyone concerned is here." He broke the seal on the envelope and read the will, which was mercifully brief.

Eduardo had left his house and most of

its contents to a foundation already set up, with the proviso that any of his descendants and their families could live there, paying a modest rent. He bequeathed each of his descendants twelve pieces of art from his collection: they would draw lots for the order of choosing. The rest he left to several museums.

His liquid assets, after taxes and certain bequests in codicils, would be divided equally among his two daughters and his grandson, this in addition to trusts already set up for them and funded. Then came the codicils: he left generous sums to Pietro and his secretary, Angelina, and to his household staff. To Stone's surprise, another codicil left the Modigliani portrait to Stone and the two similar paintings, the Picasso and the Braque, to Herbie Fisher. The codicil was signed and witnessed on the afternoon of the day they had lunched there.

"And that's it," Stone said. He raised his glass. "I give you a toast: the memory of Eduardo Bianchi, who none of us who knew him will ever forget."

Everyone drank, then they chatted for a while and took their leave.

Stone saw Mary Ann to the door, where her car awaited.

"I'm relieved to have you as co-executor,"

she said. "I worried about the responsibility."

"I'm very happy to help," Stone said.

"And thank you for tonight. You've relieved some of the family tension, I think."

And then she was gone, and Stone went to bed. He had a long day ahead the following day. But he had forgotten to ask her about Dolce.

---

## 10

Dolce Bianchi used a medium brush to fill in the colors of the sketch she had drawn on the canvas. She was working in a former storeroom of the convent that she had been given as a studio when she had begun to paint again, after neglecting art for a long time. The light was good, and she had accumulated a collection of her canvases, some of which were hung in the dining hall. There was a rap on wood, and Dolce turned to find a novitiate standing in the open doorway.

"The mother superior would like to see you," the young woman said. She was eighteen or nineteen and quite beautiful. Dolce resolved to paint her portrait.

"Thank you," Dolce said, and left her brush to soak. She wiped her hands on a cloth, brushed her hair, and left the studio, walking through the convent's garden to the small administrative wing. The secretary at work outside the office looked up and nodded for her to go in.

The mother superior, a woman in her early sixties, six feet tall and painfully thin, was working at her computer when Dolce entered. She waved Dolce to a seat without taking her eyes from the screen, then tapped in a few more words, closed the document, and turned to face Dolce.

Her mien was different today from her usual brisk but pleasant self; she seemed sad. "Dolce," she said. "My dear, I have just received an e-mail from your sister, Anna Maria, which tells me that yesterday, your father had a stroke and passed to God peacefully a few hours later."

Dolce felt a pang in her chest that she would not have expected in the circumstances. She was unable to speak.

"Your father was ninety-four years old," the mother superior said. "He lived a long and abundantly fruitful life and was true to himself and his God."

"Thank you, Mother," Dolce managed to say.

"Your father and I have had a considerable correspondence since you came to be with us. He was very pleased to hear of your recovery from your illness and hoped he might see you again."

Dolce managed a wry smile. "Thank you for telling me that," she said. She had her own collection of letters from her father, which had always been warm and affection-ate.

"I believe the time has come for you to leave us," the mother superior said. "I believe you to be in every way fit to rejoin the outside world and to make your way there."

Dolce smiled. "I think you are right," she said.

"What do you think you will do?"

"I have given that a great deal of thought," Dolce replied. "I think I will devote myself to my painting."

"You have a remarkable gift, and I am glad to hear you wish to make a career of it." The mother superior rose from her chair and walked into a smaller room, then returned, carrying a suitcase and a purse. "These are the things you had when you came to us," she said, setting them beside Dolce's chair. She then went back into the room and returned with a thick envelope. "Your father sent ten thousand euros, in preparation for this day," she said, handing it to her. "He wanted you to know that your bank and investment accounts remain open, your credit cards, as well, and your apartment in New York has been kept ready for your return, if you wish it. Your sister said in her e-mail that there is to be a high mass at St. Patrick's Cathedral for your father next week. Where do you think you will go?"

"I will take a little while to re-accustom myself to the outside world," Dolce said. "Then decide."

"As you wish, my dear." She came around the desk and embraced Dolce.

"Thank you for your many kindnesses, Mother," Dolce said, then she picked up her case and her purse and left the room.

She stopped in the sun-filled garden and sat on a bench for a few minutes, letting her heart return to its normal beat, then she took a cell phone from her apron pocket and called American Express Centurion Travel.

A few hours later, a chauffeur-driven Mercedes met Dolce at the front gate and the driver put her case into the trunk while she settled into the rear seat. "Take me to the Grand Hotel Villa Igiea," she said.

After an hour-long drive along the coast, the car arrived at the old castle, now one of Palermo's premier hotels. Her travel agent had arranged everything: she checked into a spacious and beautiful suite and looked at her spa appointments. She was hungry, and there was time for lunch.

She was given a table on the terrace, overlooking the marina and the sea beyond. She had pasta with seafood and half a bottle of wine and reflected on her time at the convent.

She had been in nearly a catatonic state when she arrived, and it took a week of tender care to revive her. During her second week there a handsome Irishman arrived and introduced himself as Frank Donovan, a priest and a psychiatrist, who had been sent to Palermo for several months to treat a bishop who had been discovered to have a woman and two children in a village outside the city, near the convent. He would be a daily visitor for her first three months, and it took only a short time for Dolce to corrupt him. To her surprise, she found him to be no virgin, and a skillful and affectionate lover. Most of her two-hour sessions with him were, thereafter, conducted in bed.

The mother superior caught on before long, and Father Frank disappeared from her life. He paid one final visit, supervised, and told her that his patient, the bishop, had recovered and that he, himself, was being sent to the Vatican to become private secretary to a highly placed cardinal, who was in charge of the Vatican Bank.

When Father Frank said goodbye, he pressed the cell phone into her hand, along with a note with a phone number, so they had stayed in touch.

Now, over her espresso, Dolce called him. "I'm out," she said.

"Wonderful! Come to Rome."

"My father has died, and I must go to New York. Can you come there?"

"Not for at least a week," he said. "It will take me that long to invent some business there."

She gave him her address on the Upper East Side. "Bring civilian clothes," she said.

He laughed. "I doubt if I will need much in the way of clothing."

"You are quite right, but we will need to leave the apartment sometimes." She said goodbye and headed for the spa.

Four days later, refreshed and carrying a new wardrobe in new luggage, Dolce arrived at JFK Airport in New York and was driven to her Park Avenue apartment. The doorman greeted her warmly and took her luggage upstairs.

Dolce settled back into her spacious apartment and began to plot her return.

# 11

Stone and Herbie arrived at the Bianchi house to find a large team of catalogers and art experts swarming over the place, with the exception of Eduardo's study, which Stone had left locked. He greeted the team, then unlocked the study door and let himself and Herbie in, then locked it behind him.

"What do you want to do today?" Herbie asked.

"I want to search this room thoroughly for hidden compartments."

"Why do you think there are hidden compartments?"

"Because Mary Ann was searching the desk for one when we found her here. Maybe she knows something we don't. Let's start with the desk."

They had been at work for, perhaps, ten minutes when Herbie found the compartment in the desk, simply by pressing on a

66

panel in the kneehole that sprang open. "It's not so hard to find hidden compartments when you know they're there somewhere," he said.

"What's inside it?" Stone asked.

Herbie swept the compartment with his hand. "Nothing," he said.

The two of them spent the remainder of the morning searching every nook of the study, then gave up and had the lunch Pietro had brought them.

"What did you think Eduardo might have been hiding?" Herbie asked.

"Evidence of holdings not mentioned in his will or financial statement. Eduardo had the house, the art, and investment accounts worth ninety million dollars managed by Mary Ann, nothing else."

"Ninety million is a pretty nice estate."

"It wasn't just about the money for Eduardo. He wanted power and influence, more than ninety million would buy."

"And you think Mary Ann knows about these holdings?"

"Somebody had to know — she's the logical guess." Stone slapped his forehead. "I forgot to tell you the news."

"What news?"

"You remember when Eduardo gave us the tour the other day, and you admired what you thought were two Picassos?"

"But one was a Braque? Sure, I remember."

"That afternoon, before his stroke, Eduardo wrote a codicil to his will that left you those two pictures."

Herbie burst out laughing. "Are you kidding me?"

"Nope, and the estate will pay the taxes. He left me the Modigliani portrait."

"Well, congratulations to us, I guess," Herbie said.

There was a rap on the study door.

"Come in!" Stone shouted. A woman wearing an artist's smock and carrying a clipboard came into the room. "Excuse me, Mr. Barrington, Mr. Fisher," she said, "but we've discovered something you should know about. Would you come with me, please?"

Stone and Herbie followed the woman into the large dining room. There were four blank spaces where pictures had hung, and the four were out of their frames and spread out on a green baize cloth over the dining table: a Matisse, a Toulouse-Lautrec, and two Blue Period Picassos.

"These four paintings are fakes," the woman said.

Stone stepped forward and looked more

closely. "Impossible. I know these pictures, they've been in the Bianchi collection for years."

"Nevertheless," she said. "They are brilliant fakes, but fakes all the same. Look at this." She turned over the Toulouse-Lautrec, pointed to a place on the canvas frame, and handed Stone a magnifying glass. "Have a look."

Stone looked at the spot. "I don't see anything but the grain of the wood," he said.

"Look more closely. I'll point it out for you." She held a pencil point at the spot.

Stone looked again. "Oh, I see it, it's a check mark. How does that make it a fake?"

"It is a check mark, from a dye, tapped into the frame's wood. It is the trademark of an art forger named Charles Magnussen."

"Why would a man go to all the trouble to forge a painting, then put a trademark on it?"

"Pride, I suppose. Magnussen died last year, but on his deathbed he told the dealer who sold his original works about the trademark. The Metropolitan discovered two Renoirs about a month ago that bore the check marks."

"First of all," Stone said, "you are bound by your contract to keep this information

69

confidential.

"Second, I want you to examine every painting and drawing in this house for the presence of that trademark and any other signs that any of the works might be forged."

"As you wish. I'll put my people to work on it."

"And, if you would, please examine that Modigliani and the Picasso and the Braque below it." He pointed. "Do those first."

Stone led Herbie back into the study.

"I don't understand," Herbie said, "Eduardo willed his collection and the house to this foundation mentioned in the will, so there would be no taxes to pay on the art. Do you think Eduardo was bilked?"

"Possibly," Stone said. "On the other hand, maybe he had the paintings copied and sold the originals — although I think that is extremely unlikely."

An hour later, the woman came into the study again. "We've carefully examined the three paintings, and it is our conviction that they are all genuine."

"Thank you," Stone said. "Please continue with your work."

"Whew!" Herbie said when she had gone.

Stone had to laugh.

By the end of the day Stone and Herbie had finished examining every object, cupboard, drawer, and book in Eduardo's study and had found nothing of import. The art expert walked through the open door.

"Mr. Barrington, we have found twenty-four forgeries of artwork in the house, nearly all of them by Magnussen and nearly all of them from the cream of the collection. It will take us another couple of days to examine the rest of the collection."

"Do you need more help?"

"I have already invited two experts on art forgery to join us, and they will be here tomorrow."

"Good. May I have a copy of the list of the twenty-four forgeries?"

She tore a page from her legal pad and handed it to him. "I've already made copies for our purposes."

"Remember, this information is highly confidential," Stone said. "There may be a logical reason for the presence of the copies in the collection."

"Of course." She left the room.

Stone laid the list of forgeries on Eduardo's desk and picked up the phone. "Now I have to call Mary Ann."

"Why?" Herbie asked. "Isn't that premature, until we know more?"

"Mary Ann may already know all we need to know."

# 12

Ann Keaton sat in an office in the Executive Office Building, across from the West Wing, and methodically worked her way through a stack of mail that had already been seen by two other senior staffers. Each had a note stapled to it recommending an action of one kind or another. The one in her hand carried the notation: *Decline — person rumored to have Mafia connections.* The handwritten letter to Kate was from Mary Ann Bianchi, a name that meant nothing to her. The name of the "person," however, had a very familiar ring. Ann gathered up the mail she had already approved for Kate's eyes, put the Bianchi letter on top of the pile, and went next door to where Kate Lee sat at a big desk, leaning back in her chair, her trousered legs on the desk, reading documents. "Hey," she said to Ann, "what've you got?"

"Standard stuff," Ann said. "Except for

the one on top."

"Ooh," Kate said when she had read the note. "I read the obit in the *Times.* Tell 'em I'll be there."

"You saw the staff recommendation?"

"Sure, I saw it. Tell Mary Ann I'll be there, to save me a seat."

"Let's think about this one more time," Ann said.

"Ann, do you remember the cocktail party that kick-started my campaign? The one where twenty-one people gave me a check for a million dollars each?"

"Of course, but I don't remember Eduardo Bianchi being there."

"He was there, without being there," Kate said.

"Maybe that's how you should attend his funeral."

"No, I'm going to attend his funeral in person, dressed in black, looking sorrowful, because that's how I'm going to feel. When you call Mary Ann, tell her I'd be very grateful if I could sit in the family pew. Eduardo didn't have that big a family — maybe I can flesh it out a little bit."

"Yes, ma'am," Ann said, rising to go.

"Ann, sit down." Ann sat.

"Eduardo Bianchi did things for me when I was at the Agency, and afterward, that nobody else could have done. He could make a phone call and find out stuff it would have taken us a year to unearth. He once got an Agency officer back from a kidnapping by the Naples Mafia, in less than four hours. He was a patriot and my dear friend, and that's what I'm going to say when somebody sticks a microphone in my face and asks me what I'm doing there. As for the Mafia business, I suggest you read Eduardo's FBI file."

"I don't have that on my desk," Ann replied. "What does it say?"

"A great deal, but absolutely nothing about the Mafia."

"Can I tell the press that?"

"Certainly not. You're not supposed to know what's in anybody's FBI file. Anybody asks, tell 'em to make a Freedom of Information request for it."

"If they do that, will they get the file?"

"Not in my lifetime," Kate replied. "Maybe not in yours."

She made a shooing motion with her hand, then went back to reading documents. "Wait," she said, as Ann reached the door.

Ann stopped.

"Call all the lawyers in the Twenty-one group and ask each of them to give me a list of five names who they think would make a sensational Supreme Court justice, along with not more than five hundred words saying why. And tell them there'd better not be more than two white men on their lists."

"Yes, ma'am."

Kate smiled. "It'll give you an excuse for calling Stone."

Ann laughed, then she stopped. "Why now? Is there a justice with a really bad cold?"

"I saw one at a cocktail party not so long ago who looked like he might not finish his martini. As Fats Waller used to say, 'One never knows, do one?'"

Ann returned to her office and called Stone's cell number. "Well, hello there," Stone said. "To what do I owe the honor?"

"This is official business of the office of the President-Elect of the United States of America."

"Oh, that. I was hoping you were in town and wanting to get laid."

"Next week, maybe, if you play your cards right."

"That's good news. I can't wait."

"There are only about two hundred things that could go wrong, so don't count on it."

"I'll hold my breath."

"Now, to business: Kate would like you to submit the names of five people who you believe would make a very fine Supreme Court justice. She would like no more than five hundred words in support of each of them, and no more than two may be white males. Got it?"

"Is somebody over at the Court looking a little peaked?"

"Who knows? I think she's just being prepared — it's in her nature."

"Okay, when?"

"Soon. Fax them to me. You already have the number."

"I'll give it some thought. Tell me, is your reason for coming up here that Kate is coming to Eduardo Bianchi's high mass at St. Patrick's?"

"She is, and she told me to ask his daughter if she can sit in the family pew."

"I'll take care of that for you, if you like."

"Thank you, I'd appreciate that. It seems like rather a personal request for me to be making to someone I don't know."

"Consider it done."

"Okay, I have to get back to work here, the paper level is rising around me."

"Right. See ya."

"Oh, Stone, one other thing."

"Yes?"

"Who the hell is Fats Waller?"

# 13

Stone got Mary Ann Bianchi on the phone. "Good day, Mary Ann."

"And to you, Stone."

"Katharine Lee's office has asked me to respond on her behalf to your invitation to Eduardo's mass. She will be there, and she would very much like to sit with the family, if you agree."

"We'd be delighted to have Kate with us," Mary Ann replied.

"I'll pass that on," Stone said. "Be prepared for a Secret Service presence."

"I'm sure St. Pat's has handled that before."

"There's another matter, concerning the estate."

"What is it?"

"Are you acquainted with the name 'Charles Magnussen'?"

"Yes, he's an art restorer, by common consent, one of the best in the world."

"Has he had, to your knowledge, any contact with Eduardo's collection?"

"Yes, he restored a number of canvases in the collection over the years. Magnussen and Papa were old friends."

"To your knowledge, did Magnussen do the restorations at Eduardo's house or in his own studio?"

"In his own studio. A painting usually took some weeks to restore."

"Are you acquainted with a tiny check mark stamped on the frames of some of the canvases he restored?"

"I've never noticed anything like that."

"Before he died last year, Magnussen told the dealer who represented him for his original works that he had forged numerous paintings and had stamped the check mark on his forgeries. Yesterday, the art catalogers at the house discovered four paintings in the collection that bore the tiny stamp. I asked them to examine all the paintings and drawings in the house for signs of forgery, and their total now stands at twenty-four oils and watercolors that carry Magnussen's check mark. They are all among the finest and most highly valued work in the collection."

Mary Ann seemed to be caught in a stunned silence.

"Are you still there?" Stone asked.

"Yes," she said hoarsely, "I'm here. You seem to be telling me that Magnussen copied the paintings while he was supposed to be restoring them."

"That is a very strong possibility. What's more, if he restored them first, then copied them, the copies would bear the same signs of restoration as the originals, making them virtually impossible to tell apart."

"My God," she breathed, "you're talking about work that probably exceeds hundreds of millions of dollars in value, at today's auction prices."

"I don't doubt it."

"Then I should call the police," she said. "They have an art squad that deals with this sort of thing."

"I think it would be better if you let me pursue the matter privately — at least, at first."

"How would you go about that?"

"I know Magnussen's dealer. He found me two of my mother's paintings, which I bought."

"Is he the sort of person who would know how to dispose of such work as Papa's collection?"

"I should think so, he's eminent in his field. I should say, however, that his reputation is beyond reproach. I don't think he's the sort of man who would participate in such a crime. Still, I should talk to him, representing the estate."

"Please do that, Stone, and quickly. We can't have word of this getting out."

"I'll try and call you tomorrow," Stone said. He said goodbye and hung up.

Stone got into his jacket and an overcoat and stopped by Joan's desk. "I'm going out for a while," he said to her. "You can reach me on my cell."

"Have fun," she said.

Stone walked to Park Avenue, then to Fifty-seventh Street, where he went west to a large building near Carnegie Hall. The name, etched into the granite facade, read THE PITT GALLERY. He went inside, gave his name, and asked to see Raoul Pitt. He was asked to wait for a few minutes, and a young woman took his coat. He browsed among the expensive paintings and sculptures on display for a few minutes, then Raoul Pitt appeared with another man. They shook hands, and the man left.

"Hello, Stone," Pitt said, shaking his hand warmly. "Would you like to come back to my office?"

"Thank you, Raoul, yes." Stone followed him to the rear of the building and his large, sparsely furnished office, which overlooked a sculpture garden out back. Pitt made them both a cup of espresso from a little machine, then sat down in a chair facing Stone.

"Well, now, what can I do for you today, Stone?"

"I've come to see you about your late client, Charles Magnussen."

"Ah, Charles," Pitt said regretfully. "A very fine painter."

"And, from all accounts, a very fine forger," Stone said. "I've heard the story about the check marks he placed on the frames of his forgeries."

Pitt shook his head. "I was shocked when he told me of that in the hospital. He died two days later. How did you hear?"

"I'm co-executor for the Eduardo Bianchi estate," Stone said. "One of the people cataloging his collection told me about it."

"Ah, Eduardo. I sold him a few things over the years, but he usually bought at auction, always by proxy. And before bidding, he sent his own experts to examine the works and pronounce them genuine."

"Twenty-four of the paintings in Eduardo's collection bear the tiny check marks that Magnussen told you about."

"Good God!" Pitt exhaled. He looked ill. "What a catastrophe!"

"Eduardo hired Magnussen as a restorer," Stone said. "Probably right after he got out of prison. He did what, eight, ten years for art forgery?"

"Something like that. I can see where this is going. You're saying Charles took the works to his studio, restored, then copied them to include the marks of restoration."

"Something like that."

Pitt shook his head. "I hope you have taken steps to see that word does not get out. The consequences for the art market could be devastating. There are always rumors floating around the world, saying that one multimillion-dollar painting or another sold at auction was a forgery. This news could make things worse."

"I had hoped that, with your help, the original paintings might be recovered before that happens." He handed Pitt a copy of the cataloger's list.

Pitt read it. "I'll do whatever I can to help," he said. "May I make a suggestion?"

"Of course."

"I think you should send the team working at Eduardo's house here, to my gallery and the eight floors of storage space upstairs. I will assign staff to help them view every painting in the place for signs of forgery. I do not ever want it suggested that

I sold these pictures or had any part in this."

"Good idea," Stone said. "I'll send them to you. In the meantime, if you could put a couple of people to work going through auction catalogs for the past twenty years, to see if anything on the list came up for sale."

"That will be a huge job," Pitt said. "May I hire extra help at the expense of the estate?"

"Yes, you may." Stone stood up and shook the man's hand. "I'll be in touch."

Stone retrieved his coat, left the gallery, and took a cab home. This, he thought, was going to be a mess.

# 14

Stone and Dino met for dinner at a new restaurant, the Writing Room, which was located in the old Elaine's premises on the Upper East Side, at Second Avenue and Eighty-eighth Street. It was their first time there, and they walked into a place that was unrecognizable as the site of the old joint.

The bar had been moved into the smaller of the two main rooms, and the new dining room was much larger than the old. They were greeted as old friends by the new owners and seated in the rear room, designed as a library.

"Where did they find the space for this room?" Stone asked.

"This was the outdoor space where the garbage cans were kept," Dino said. "Not bad, huh?"

Their drinks arrived unbidden. At least that hadn't changed.

"Something's come up," Stone said.

"Tell me."

"A crime may have been committed, but I'm not sure yet."

"Well, I'm the police — tell me."

"You can't treat this as a crime, until I know more."

"Come on, Stone, give."

"It looks as though twenty-four of the best paintings in Eduardo's collection are forgeries."

Dino choked on his drink. "Impossible," he was finally able to say. "Nobody could get a forgery past Eduardo, let alone two dozen."

"That's not how it happened. Eduardo hired a well-known art restorer to work on these pictures. It looks as though he returned forgeries to Eduardo. Since they were all supposed to be restorations, Eduardo may have been taken in. At ninety-four, his eyesight might not have been what it was."

"What have you done about this?"

"I went to see Raoul Pitt." Stone told him about the check marks. "He's very concerned, and he wants the estate to audit all the paintings in his studio and in storage, so that no one will suspect him of being involved."

"Does anybody outside the family know

about this?"

"Only Mary Ann knows — I had to tell her. The others have no idea, and at some point, Mary Ann, Ben — plus Dolce, if she's capable — are supposed to choose twelve pictures each as part of their inheritance. The others are supposed to be left in the house. Eduardo wanted arts organizations to be able to bring small groups to view the collection."

"How good are the forgeries?"

"The forger, one Charles Magnussen, had a long history of making undetectable copies of paintings. He was finally nailed and did some time. After that, he made his living as a restorer. I guess he finally had a conscience at the end, because he told Raoul on his deathbed about the check marks. When word gets out, collectors all over the world are going to be taking a magnifying glass to their canvas frames."

"Anything I can do to help in all this?"

"Just keep your mouth shut for the time being. I'll let you know when to turn it over to the art squad."

"Whatever you say."

Their dinner arrived, and they pronounced it pretty good.

Riding home in Dino's departmental armored SUV, Dino took a deep breath and let it out slowly. "I can think of another scenario with these pictures," he said. "I feel bad about even bringing it up."

"Go on."

"When the searching starts for the originals, you're going to have to take a look in Mary Ann's town house."

Stone was shocked. "Are you kidding me?"

"I hope I'm wrong, but she's avaricious enough to want them for herself, instead of touring groups of art lovers. After all, those people are not going to know the difference between an original and a forgery. She thinks that way."

"I can't believe she'd do that."

"Look at it from her point of view: she would figure she's not hurting anybody, and if the secret didn't get out, she might someday be able to sell some of them privately, or just leave them to Ben."

"I was just thinking this afternoon that this is going to be a terrible fucking mess, but if Mary Ann is involved, it's going to be exponentially worse."

"Not necessarily," Dino said.

"What are you talking about?"

"Mary Ann is smart enough to have a way out of this. If she gets caught, she can just give the pictures back and it would all be kept in the family. No one would want the

88

publicity that would come from prosecuting her."

"You have a serpentine mind, Dino."

"Not I — Mary Ann. Trust me, she has a *very* serpentine mind. She was always a step ahead of me."

"You know, when I think about it, this might be the most favorable explanation."

"Favorable?"

"In the sense of resolving it while making the fewest waves."

"Careful, Mary Ann will be one step ahead of you, too."

# 15

Stone was at his desk the following morning, working on the Bianchi estate financial statement, prior to giving it to the accountants to help them prepare a final tax return for Eduardo and an estate tax return.

Joan buzzed. "There's a guy on the phone who says he has some important information for you, but he won't give his name."

"How crazy does he sound?"

"Not very."

"Oh, all right." He pressed the other line button. "This is Stone Barrington. Who's this?"

"I can't tell you that now, Mr. Barrington — maybe later. A meeting took place last night in Washington, and what was discussed there has shocked me to the core."

"What kind of meeting?"

"I guess you could call it a strategy session," the man said.

"Who attended?"

"About two dozen Republican senators and congressmen. It was held at a private residence in Georgetown."

"Were you there?"

There was a long pause. "Let's just say that I have an intimate knowledge of what was discussed."

"What was discussed?"

"Henry Carson was the de facto chairman. He shared the chair with the about-to-become-former Speaker of the House. These people are extremely angry about losing the presidency and furious about not having control of either House."

"Are you a Republican, Mr. . . . ?"

"I'd rather not say which party I belong to."

"Go on, tell me what transpired."

"Carson spoke to the group, and he was right up front. He said the party strategy in Congress would be to oppose and obstruct — he actually used those words — every bill that was introduced by the new administration, and they would issue talking points to the group about what to say to the press and media when the new administration announced policy initiatives."

"Every bill? Every policy? No matter what?"

"Every single one. They said they would

find ways to peck to death any bill or policy. The rationale for each set of talking points will be created and laid out in the circulated memo."

"Well, that shocks me, too," Stone said. "They don't even know what policy initiatives she's going to issue."

"They can guess from Mrs. Lee's campaign speeches."

"What do you want me to do with this information?" Stone asked.

"I want you to get it into the press and media. I want to create a big to-do about this, and I want to blunt their tactics."

"Those are noble aims," Stone said, "but you're going about this in the wrong way."

"Then how should I go about it?"

"Do you have a pencil?" Stone rummaged in a desk drawer for a business card.

"Yes."

"Write down this name and number: Carla Fontana. She's the Washington bureau chief for the *New York Times.*" He gave the man a number. "That is her private cell number. She's in a position to do what you're suggesting, but you have to understand, she's going to have to know who she's dealing with."

"I'm afraid of talking to someone like that on the phone," the man said.

"Then do this: go to an electronics store and buy two prepaid cell phones. Mail her one with a note saying you will call her at a specified hour, and that if she takes your call, you'll have a major story for her. The phones will be untraceable, and if you're worried about taps, you can always throw them away and buy new ones."

"That sounds good."

"But she's going to need to know your identity. Will she recognize your name?"

"Probably."

"My advice is to be straight with her — don't lie to her and don't conceal your identity from her. She has to trust you if this is going to work."

"May I tell her you referred me to her?"

Stone thought about that. "Yes, but tell her I don't know who you are."

"All right."

"One more thing," Stone said. "I'm glad you're being careful, but are you doing that because you fear some retribution? If they find out, will they destroy your career?"

"If they find out, they may destroy more than that."

"What does that mean?"

"Thank you for your time, Mr. Barrington." The man hung up.

Stone was left staring at his phone.

# 16

Stone was picked up at home by Dino, and his driver took them to a side entrance of St. Patrick's Cathedral, where the block had been closed to provide parking for the many limousines of the attendees to the high mass for Eduardo Bianchi.

Inside, a boys' choir was singing something from Beethoven, and there was the quiet hum of influential people greeting one another.

"I'm not sitting with the family," Dino said.

"Why not?"

"I wasn't invited, and if I had been I wouldn't have accepted. It would have caused too much talk."

"See you afterward, then. Are you going to the house?"

"That, I'm doing."

"I'll ride with you, then back with the kids."

Stone walked to where the two front pews had been set aside for the family and their friends. Stone walked to where Mary Ann sat next to her son, Ben, on the aisle, in the front pew, greeted her quietly, and murmured some words of condolence. Stone took a seat in the front pew, next to his son, Peter, and his girlfriend, Hattie Patrick.

A moment later, the president-elect entered from the Fiftieth Street side of the cathedral, and Stone rose to greet her. She spoke briefly to Mary Ann, then came and sat by Stone. She squeezed his arm, then sat with her hands in her lap, her head bowed.

The cardinal had just finished his prayer when there was a small stir behind where Stone sat, and he was aware of someone taking a seat in the pew directly behind him, but he did not turn to look.

A procession of the city's prominent persons — the mayor, the chairmen of the boards of the Metropolitan Museum of Art and two other important museums, and Tom Donnelly, Dino's predecessor as police commissioner, now a candidate for mayor, all spoke of what Eduardo had meant to their work and to the city. There followed another performance by the choir, then the cardinal gave his benediction and the service ended.

Stone stood and chatted with Kate for a moment.

"Can you and your kids come to the Carlyle for dinner tonight at seven?" she asked.

"We'd love to," Stone said, then the Secret Service escorted her to where the cardinal waited to say goodbye, then led her out the way she had come — a slow process, since everyone wanted to shake her hand.

Stone turned to look at the people behind him, then froze.

Dolce was sitting quietly in the pew directly behind him. She rose and held out her hand.

"Hello, Stone," she said softly, holding out her gloved hand.

Stone took her hand. "Hello, Dolce," he said. "How are you?"

"Much better than the last time we met," she said.

Stone recalled that, on that occasion, she had been carrying a butcher knife. "I'm so glad," he said.

"Will you be coming back to the house?"

"Yes," he said.

"Perhaps we might talk for a moment there."

"Of course." She was the last person on earth he wished to speak to.

She left the pew and spoke to a few attendees. Then Mary Ann approached her, they air-kissed and spoke for only a moment.

People lingered to schmooze in the pews and aisles, but gradually the crowd dissipated, and Stone made his way back to Dino's car. Peter and Hattie got into the Bentley, with Fred at the wheel. Mary Ann and Ben were driven in a black Mercedes.

"A nice send-off, huh?" Dino said.

"Very nice. Did you see Dolce?"

"She was there?" Dino asked, alarmed.

"Sitting directly behind me."

"Jesus, if I'd known I'd have had some men there."

"She seemed . . . normal, whatever that is for Dolce. You'll see her at the house."

"Oh yeah," Dino said, "I'm really looking forward to that."

Eduardo Bianchi was interred in a mausoleum in a grove of trees behind the mansion. The cardinal prayed, and the casket was moved into the little building, then it was locked and the key given to Mary Ann.

The group of about a hundred people wandered back to the house, where a buffet had been laid out in the dining room. Stone had seen that the forgeries of Eduardo's paintings had been rehung in their original places.

"They look real to me," Dino said.

"They looked real to everybody," Stone said, "until somebody noticed that check mark on a painting's frame."

Stone had something to eat and moved around the room, speaking to those he knew. Then he looked up and saw Dolce standing in a side doorway. She crooked a finger at him and beckoned.

Stone gulped.

# 17

Stone left through the side door and stepped into the hallway. Dolce was just disappearing into Eduardo's study at the end of the hall. He walked slowly toward the study and hesitated at the doors. Finally, he figured he had to do this sometime, and it might as well be now.

He opened the door and peeked through. Dolce was sitting at her father's desk across the room. He walked into the room, leaving the door open behind him.

Dolce rose, walked around the desk and toward him. She was wearing a tight black silk dress and had removed her hat and veil. She held out both her hands for Stone to take.

Stone liked the idea of her not having a free hand and took them both in his. She presented a cheek to be kissed, and he complied.

"A long time," she said.

Not long enough, Stone thought. "Yes. I'm glad you've fared well."

She took back her hands, walked to the sofa, and sat down. Stone took a chair next to her.

"The convent provided me with psychiatric care," she said. "Gradually, I became myself again."

Stone shuddered at the thought of who that might be. "I'm glad."

"I want to apologize to you for my behavior in the past," she said. "I can only claim insanity as a defense — and that, I have found, can be cured."

"What are your plans?" Stone asked.

"Thank you for sending me the will and the codicils," she said. "I'm going to take advantage of Papa's generosity once more and move into this house, into his room, in fact. A little redecoration, and it will suit me perfectly. There's an old stone barn out back in the woods, near the mausoleum. I'm going to turn it into a studio and paint."

He hadn't sent her the will, and he supposed that Mary Ann had. "I didn't know you painted," Stone said, trying to keep the conversation moving.

"I did as a girl, and I showed talent. I had time to develop that talent in Sicily, and now I want to make a career."

"That sounds like a good idea."

"Thank you. Stone, I know that we cannot be lovers again, but I hope we can be friends."

Stone looked doubtful. "I'm seeing someone who is important to me, and I don't think she would be happy with our being friends."

"Cordial old acquaintances, then."

"Of course."

She rose. "Have we anything else to say to each other?"

"I have only to wish you well — most sincerely."

"Then I'd better return to our guests," she said, and preceded him out of the study.

Stone followed her at a distance, breathing large sighs of relief.

When he got to the living room, Kate Lee had arrived, and Ann Keaton was with her. Ann smiled and took a step toward him, but he raised a finger, stopping her in her tracks. *Later,* he mouthed. She turned back to her previous conversation.

Mary Ann approached him. "Did you speak with Dolce?"

"Yes."

"I wasn't expecting her. How did she seem?"

He almost said "Normal," but that was a

stretch. "Composed," he replied. "She said she had seen the will, and she's going to move into this house and take Eduardo's bedroom, then she's going to renovate an old stone barn out back and use it for a studio for her painting."

"She painted as a girl, and beautifully."

"I think it's good that she has something to keep her busy."

"Thank God for that, I'd hate to have to keep her amused."

"She said she had psychiatric treatment in the convent."

"Papa told me that, though he didn't tell me much."

"Do you have any problem with her living in this house?"

"If I did, would it matter? Certainly, I don't want to live here, and Ben is in California. How is it going with the estate?"

"Eduardo's final personal tax return and the estate return have been filed. Progress toward probate seems smooth."

"How much in estate taxes?" she asked.

"Fifty million, give or take. You, Ben, and Dolce will get more than ten million each, taxes paid. Think you can squeak by on that?"

She laughed, something she didn't do often. "I guess we'll have to," she said.

Gradually, the crowd thinned, and Stone walked out of the house with Kate and Ann.

"See you at seven," Kate said. "Oh, and bring Dino and Viv."

"Viv's away on business, as she often is, but I'm sure Dino would be delighted. May he bring his son, Ben, and his girl, if they're free?"

"Of course." She got into a waiting government SUV.

Stone pulled Ann aside. "I'm sorry we couldn't talk earlier," he said. "I'll explain later." She followed Kate into the car and was gone.

Stone had a word with Dino about the evening, then he got into the Bentley with Peter and Hattie and was driven home.

# 18

Stone arrived at the Carlyle on time and found Dino, Ben, and Tessa waiting in the lobby. He identified his party to the Secret Service agent on duty, and they were whisked up to the Lees' penthouse apartment.

A maid opened the door, then Kate greeted them all warmly, remembering everybody's name. A butler took their drinks order, and Ann came out of a bedroom and joined them.

Stone took her aside. "This afternoon I had just concluded a meeting with Dolce, Eduardo's younger daughter, and I didn't want her to see us talking."

"Is this the crazy one?"

"Was and may still be, for all I know."

"The one who tried to kill you?"

"Unsuccessfully."

"Thank you for not pointing me out to her," Ann said, laughing. "Wasn't that a spectacular house?"

"It certainly is. I've been working there for a week, getting the estate ready for probate."

"I want to hear all about Eduardo, when you have a chance."

"Before I get into that, there's something I have to talk with you and Kate about privately."

"Give me a few minutes, and I'll cut her out of the herd."

They rejoined the others, got their drinks, and all was convivial.

A few minutes later, Stone saw Ann and Kate walk into a bedroom. Ann beckoned with her chin, and he followed. He found Kate stretched out on the bed and Ann sitting at the foot, on a bench.

"What's up?" Ann asked.

Stone pulled up a chair. "Yesterday I got an anonymous phone call from a man who told me that he had intimate knowledge of a meeting in a private house in Georgetown attended by Henry Carson, the Speaker, and a couple of dozen Republicans from both Houses of Congress."

"Any idea who your caller was?"

"Not the slightest. He wouldn't say if he actually attended the meeting or even if he was a Republican, but he was shocked by what he heard."

Kate raised her head from the bed. "What shocked him?"

"It seems the purpose of the meeting was to agree on a plan to block every bill you send to Congress and every policy initiative you put forward."

Kate sat up and put her feet on the floor. "But they don't know what those are."

"Apparently, it doesn't matter what they are."

Kate shook her head. "I didn't know Honk hated me."

"The caller says they're all angry about losing the presidency and furious about not having control of either House, so it may not have been personal."

"What did the man want of you?" Ann asked.

"He wanted me to get the story to the press."

"And did you?"

"I gave him Carla Fontana's cell number and told him to call her. I also told him that his story wouldn't be credible if he refused to identify himself."

"And this was yesterday?" Kate asked.

"Yes. I advised him to buy two throwaway cell phones and send one to Carla, so it may take him a day or two to accomplish that."

"Ann," Kate said, "has Carla been sniffing around?"

"Yes," Ann replied, "along with everybody else in the White House Press Corps."

"If she calls you, take her call," Kate said. "Anything else, Stone?"

"No."

She stood up. "Then let me buy you another drink before dinner." She took his arm and walked back into the living room. "By the way," she whispered, "you did the right thing."

They sat down to dinner at seven forty-five and were served foie gras, Dover sole, and crème brûlée. After dinner they were arrayed around the living room, having coffee and after-dinner drinks, when Ann's cell phone apparently vibrated, because she removed it from a skirt pocket, looked at who the caller was, then left the room. Ten minutes later, she beckoned Stone and Kate to join her. They went to the bedroom again.

"That was Carla Fontana," she said. "Stone, your anonymous caller has made contact and has told her the same story he told you."

"Did she find out who he was?"

"She's going to rendezvous with him sometime tomorrow, and he promises all will be revealed."

"Will she be in touch with you?" Kate asked.

"She didn't actually say so, but that was my impression."

"Then we shall see what we shall see," Kate said.

They all went back to the party.

# 19

Stone was half asleep when the security system began to beep. He glanced at the bedside telephone display and saw the message: "Front door open." He entered his code, and the beeping stopped. He lay quietly, waiting.

She came into the room, and he heard the sound of a zipper, then of clothes falling to the floor. Ann landed on the bed as if from a great height. "And a very good evening to you!" she shouted.

Stone grabbed her and pulled her to him. "You're not treating your clothes very well."

"I was in a hurry. I'm getting laid."

"You certainly are," he replied, kicking off his covers.

She hugged him to her breast. "God, it seems like a year since I felt a man next to me."

"It's less than a month," he said, tickling her lightly between the legs. She immediately became wet, and he climbed aboard.

"And just as long since I've felt that weight," she said.

He slid slowly inside her, and she made a happy noise. "And years since I've felt that!"

"Tell me how it feels," he said softly, moving slowly in and out.

"Heavenly. Are you an angel or a devil?"

"A little of both," he breathed.

She ran her nails down his back. "Oh, how I've missed you."

"And I, you."

"And how I've missed this!"

"How long can we do this before you abandon me again?" he asked, but he didn't stop.

"Forever, if I quit my job."

"But you're not going to quit, are you?"

"What can I say? My country needs me. I have to be back at the Carlyle, looking unfucked, by seven AM."

Stone increased the pace, and they stopped talking and concentrated. She climaxed three times before she pushed him off.

"A girl's gotta rest," she said.

Stone laid his head on her breasts and rubbed her belly.

She slapped his hand. "Don't get me started again," she said. "At least, not for a few minutes. When I can make a fist again, I'll entertain you."

Stone rolled onto his back and she rested her hand on him. "God, how I love a stick shift," she said, kissing it.

"Talk to me," he said. "Tell me what it's like for you these days."

She didn't let go, but managed to talk. "Exciting, exhausting, exciting, exhausting. That's it, both at the same time."

"What's been your biggest surprise?"

"How exciting it is. It's like the campaign to the nth!"

"And your biggest disappointment?"

"That I can't stay awake and do the job twenty-four hours a day."

"So, you're happy in your work?"

"Not so much happy as elated."

"What's the difference?"

"Elated is like watching your team score, knowing that they can't score on every play. Happy would be if they could score whenever they feel like it. And we all know that's not going to happen."

"How's Will taking the transition?"

"Oh, Will is always Will: cheerful, optimistic. He would have been here for the funeral, but he's meeting with the Japanese prime minister in Los Angeles. Will has a surprise for him."

"What surprise?"

"Will has gotten some contributors to donate a statue honoring the Japanese-Americans who were interned during the big war."

"That's good of him."

"I think he's doing it for Franklin Roosevelt. He said when he meets Roosevelt in heaven he wants to tell him that he did what he could to right the wrong."

"That's a very fine motive."

"The words on the statue are 'They also served and sacrificed.' "

"Perfect."

"I'm elated, but it's still tough," Ann said. "I came real close to starting smoking again."

"When did you quit?"

"Fifteen years ago."

"And you still want it?"

"Sometimes. Why? Would that be a deal breaker?"

"You know my friends — have you ever seen one of them smoke?"

"Now that you mention it."

"I'm not a fanatic about it," Stone said. "As far as I'm concerned, there are only two places where it should be banned."

"Where are they?"

"Indoors and outdoors."
She laughed until he pounced again.

# 20

Ann woke him at five AM and attacked him. Stone submitted gracefully. Done with him, she jumped into a shower, pulled a change of clothes from her large handbag, replacing them with those worn, spent half an hour doing something with a hair dryer in the bathroom, then woke up Stone again.

"There's a car waiting for me downstairs. I can't stay for breakfast."

"Look in the dumbwaiter," Stone said, pointing.

Ann looked and found a brown paper bag. "What's in it?"

"Some of Helene's pastries and coffee. You can enjoy it on the way to the Carlyle. Will I ever see you again short of the inauguration?"

"Of course," she said, kissing him, "but as Rodgers and Hart once said, 'Who knows where or when?' "

"I'll wait with bated breath."

She kissed him and ran from the room. Stone fell asleep again.

Stone was working in his office with Herbie after lunch when his cell phone buzzed on his belt. "Hello?"

"It's Carla Fontana," she said.

"Good afternoon, Carla. I hope you're well."

"I am, thank you, and better than ever, thanks to your referral."

"Did he prove cooperative?"

"I met him an hour ago in the rear office of an antiques shop on Pennsylvania Avenue, in Georgetown."

"And?"

"He was very cooperative. He told me his name, and he said I could tell you."

"Who is he?"

"He is Evan Hills, a first-term Republican congressman from Pennsylvania, and he was very brave. He knows that if his leadership ever finds out he spoke to me, he'll be gutted and hung out to dry, and I think he actually believes they'll have him killed."

"Who's 'they'?"

"Some dark figure or other. Who knows?"

"Is it a story?"

"Is it ever! Evan has an excellent memory, and he was able to give me a verbatim account of who said what. He made notes as soon as he got home."

"Whose house was the meeting held at?"

"Ready for this? Harley David, oil billionaire who's backed a dozen right-wing organizations. He has a son, Junior, who's known as Harley Davidson — get it?"

"The poor kid."

"No, he's a rotten little bully. He drives around Dallas and D.C. in a Ferrari, mowing down pedestrians. He's had two hit-and-runs in Texas while drinking and has walked away from both, leaving a trail of his daddy's money in his wake."

"He sounds like a charmer."

"Not only that, but his daddy is clearing the way for a congressional seat for him next time."

"Was H. David Senior at the meeting?"

"He was."

"When will your story run?"

"A few days, maybe."

"Maybe?"

"I've got some checking around to do. I want to be sure that I — and you — are not being set up. This has been a little too easy. I have a list of who was at the meeting, and there's one other guy I might be able to get to cop to being there. I need a second source."

"You would know better about that than I."

"I've talked to my executive editor in New York, and he's excited, but, like me, he thinks that it may be too good to be true. The Gray Lady doesn't want her tit caught in a wringer, and Harley David would like nothing better than for that to happen. Also, I want to see what else I can get out of our man Evan Hills."

"What's Hills's background?"

"Deerfield Academy, Penn, Yale Law School, practiced with a Philadelphia white shoe firm, very Republican."

"What are his motives in all this?"

"Well you may ask. If he's for real, I think he has a conscience, and he's put off by the right-wing tilt in his party. Also, I have nothing to back this up but intuition, but I think he's gay and afraid the Republicans will shun him if he comes out."

"Does he have money?"

"He certainly appears to. His father is a big-time commodities trader, and that means he's either very rich or very poor. Evan was married once, to a girl from a very Main Line family, not the sort that would have a pauper or a Democrat for a son-in-law. They were divorced, amicably, after a couple of years."

117

"Well, I hope he turns out to be real. I can't wait to read the story in the *Times.*"

"Neither can I. Are we ever going to have that dinner we talked about in Paris?"

"Just as soon as you come to New York."

"I'll be there the day after tomorrow."

"Where are you staying?"

"With friends at One Fifth Avenue, in the Village."

"I'll have you picked up at six-thirty and brought here for a drink, then we'll go on from there." He gave her the address.

"You're on."

"So are you." They hung up. Stone buzzed Joan and asked her to have Fred collect Carla.

"That sounded interesting," Herbie said. "Who was it?"

Stone swore him to secrecy and told him the story, minus Hills's identity.

"I think it's going to be fun, following this story."

"We can only hope."

# 21

The following day Stone received word from the court that Eduardo Bianchi's estate had been released from probate, and that the proceeds could now be distributed. Stone was flabbergasted. Probate took weeks or months — in problematic cases, years.

Herbie shook his head. "It looks like Eduardo knows people who, even after his death, want to make life easier for him."

Stone called Mary Ann and told her the news. She seemed pleased but not surprised.

"Just between you and me, Mary Ann, was influence brought to bear here?"

"Nothing untoward," she replied, "so don't worry. Daddy had many friends."

"I understand. Shall we now distribute the bequests?"

"Good idea. How do we go about it?"

"I'll make up a list of all of them, and we'll meet to cosign the checks."

"Say when."

"Tomorrow at three, my office?"

"I'll see you then."

Stone hung up and turned to Herbie. "The list is your job," he said. "Do you want your associates to help?"

"I'm way ahead of you," Herbie said, taking a file folder from his briefcase and handing it to Stone.

Stone read through the document quickly. "It looks as though Eduardo's influence extends to you. Good job!"

Herbie shrugged. "I can be bought for a Picasso and a Braque. When do we get our pictures?"

"I'll send Fred out there to collect them from Pietro." He called the Bianchi house, spoke to Pietro and gave him instructions on wrapping and boxing the three pictures. He hung up. "I'll have Fred deliver them to you. Office or home?"

"They'll impress more people at the office," Herbie said.

The following day, Mary Ann arrived on time. Stone gave her a cup of tea and handed her the document to read.

"All very neatly done," she said. "And the checks?"

Stone buzzed Joan, who brought the checks, each clipped neatly to a covering letter explaining the disbursement.

"We cosign the checks and the letters," Stone said, handing her half the stack and taking the other for himself. When they were signed they traded stacks and repeated the process.

"There, all done," Stone said. "I noticed that there was no bequest to the foundation for the maintenance of the house and property."

"Papa took care of that when he set up the foundation. There's more than enough in the endowment to generate the necessary income."

"Has Dolce discussed with you her moving into the house?"

"She has, and I'm content with her wishes. She'll pay for whatever alterations she wishes to make and for the renovation of the barn, which has already started, I understand. That building predates the house by a couple of hundred years. It was damaged in a battle of the Revolutionary War. It should make a beautiful studio."

"Would you like me to overnight the disbursements or have them delivered by messenger?"

"By messenger, I think. I'll deliver Ben's to him." She stood and picked up Ben's folder. "Well, it looks as though we're all done. Thank you for handling everything so expeditiously, Stone."

Stone stood to walk her out. "There only remains the investigation into the forged paintings," he said.

"Where are we on that?"

"The audit of Raoul Pitt's gallery is nearly completed. If we don't come up with an explanation of what's happened, we'll have to turn it over to the NYPD's art squad."

"Whatever it takes," Mary Ann said.

"Oh, I sent my man, Fred, out to the house to pick up the three paintings that Eduardo bequeathed to Herb Fisher and me. Pietro is packing them."

"That's fine, one less thing to worry about."

"Does Dolce know about the forgeries?"

"Yes, and she was angry about it. She'll be anxious to hear how the investigation is going."

They said goodbye, and Stone asked Joan to messenger the letters and checks to the heirs. They were on their way in half an hour.

Fred arrived with Stone's picture, having already delivered Herbie's to his office. Joan came in with a box cutter and cut away the wrappings, and Stone set the painting on the back of the sofa, switched on all the

lights, and regarded his new treasure.
"I think I'll keep it," he said.

# 22

Dolce was tidying up her apartment in anticipation of the arrival of her guest when the phone rang. "Hello?"

"I'm in a cab," Father Frank Donovan said. "Twenty minutes, according to the driver."

"I'll have a drink waiting," she said. They hung up, and she went into the kitchen and opened the package from the liquor store: two bottles of Bushmills Black Label Irish whiskey.

She took them to the bar and filled the ice bucket from the machine.

All was ready when the bell rang. She opened the front door and threw herself into his arms. "I can't believe you're here," she said, then looked him up and down. "And in civvies!"

"I didn't want the doorman to think I'm visiting to hear your confession," Frank said. He handed her a thick envelope. "They

124

asked me to deliver this to you." He set his suitcases inside the door and closed it behind him.

She led him into the living room and tossed the envelope onto the sofa without looking at it, then went to pour them a drink.

"What a beautiful place," Frank said, looking around.

"There'll be more pictures on the walls in a day or two," she said. "I asked the convent to pack up all my work and airfreight them to me. Do you know, I've got more than sixty completed canvases, not counting the ones that weren't good enough." She handed him his drink and poured herself one, then sat on the sofa, where she encountered a lump.

"What's this?" she asked, pulling the envelope from beneath her.

"It's what the doorman asked me to deliver."

She ripped it open and read the covering letter, then looked at the check. "It appears I'm now a very rich woman," she said, waving the check. "Papa's estate has been probated."

"I congratulate you," he said, clicking his glass against hers.

"Goodness," she said, fanning herself with

the envelope. "This is going to take some getting used to." She took a swig from her drink. "I hope you have no duties but me while you're here."

"Oh, I'll have to suit up and swing by the archdiocese at some point. A courtesy call, to justify spending a week in New York."

"We have a week!"

"We do."

"Whatever will we do with ourselves?" she asked, kissing him and tugging at his necktie.

"We'll think of something," he said, kissing her back and scratching a nipple through her silk blouse.

Stone's doorbell rang, the signal from Fred Flicker that his guest was on the way up. Stone slipped into his jacket and went downstairs in time to greet Carla Fontana in the living room.

"What beautiful paneling and bookcases," Carla said, looking around.

"My father designed and built it all," Stone replied. "It was a commission from my grandmother's sister, who owned the house. She left it to me. The pictures in this room are all by my mother, Matilda Stone."

Carla looked at the pictures and took her time. "Just beautiful," she said. "Haven't I seen some of her work at the Metropolitan?"

"You have." He led her into the study and offered her a seat on the sofa. "What can I get you?"

"A martini, please. How soon you forget!" They had met a few weeks before in Paris when she had interviewed him on the occasion of the opening of the new Arrington hotel there.

"That was remiss of me," Stone said, taking a frosty bottle from the freezer and filling a martini glass. He handed it to her and poured himself a Knob Creek.

"My goodness," she said, staring at the wall next to the bar, where the Modigliani now hung. "Have you looted a museum?"

"No, that is the bequest of a friend who recently passed away."

"That would be Eduardo Bianchi?"

"How did you know?"

"Do you think I don't read my own newspaper? He had quite an obit — nearly two pages."

"He certainly did, for a man who most people didn't know existed."

"I met him once, in my publisher's office, when I was still based in New York. I remember noticing that the boss put on his jacket to receive him, which he normally did only when the president or the cardinal visited."

"Eduardo had that effect on people."

She sipped her martini. "That is the coldest thing I ever tasted."

"It's been in the freezer, waiting for you. I make martinis and gimlets by the bottle. It's easier that way."

"How does one make a gimlet?"

"One pours six ounces of vodka from a seven-hundred-and-fifty-milliliter bottle, replaces it with Rose's Sweetened Lime Juice, puts it in the freezer overnight, then serves."

"Simple enough. I'll remember that."

"Not as simple as pouring a glass of bourbon," he said.

"Where are we dining?" she asked.

"At Patroon, a few blocks from here."

"I've heard about it, never been."

"Good. Any news from your contact?"

"I'll tell you about it over dinner," she said. "For now, let's just drink."

# 23

They settled into a banquette at Patroon and ordered their second drink.

"All right," Stone said, "tell me about Deep . . . What do you call him?"

"I don't know — Deep Tonsils?"

Stone laughed.

"Let's just call him the Source."

"That'll do. Then we'll never be heard mentioning his name."

"Right, we can't do that in public. The Source and I had another meeting, same place. The antiques shop is owned by a friend of his — probably a *very* good friend. They do make a handsome couple."

"Is it a good shop?"

"It's wonderful. I've already bought a couple of things, and I have my eye on an honest-to-God Tiffany lamp, which I can't afford on my salary."

"And what did the Source have to say?"

"He brought me a typed-up copy of his

notes from the first meeting, and a list of everyone present."

"Well, *that* will add credence to your story when it runs. When will it run?"

"There is now a team, two in Washington, two in New York, running a fine-toothed comb through the details, which is not as easy as it sounds. For instance, we're trying to establish that every person there was not actually somewhere else, and we have to do that without asking the person or his or her staff. It's not easy."

"Have you developed another source who was at the meeting?"

"That's even harder. Every one of them is a rock-ribbed right winger, and none of them is inclined to be interviewed by that Great Satan, the *Times,* unless it's to defame the president or the president-elect. However, I've gotten chummy with that dazzling blond congresswoman from Georgia, Mimi Meriwether. She's a first cousin to Senator Sam Meriwether, whom you know."

"I do, and it's hard to imagine that a cousin of Sam's could be encamped on the Right. Where did she go wrong?"

"Runs in the family. Her father and his brother, Sam's father, were both Dixiecrats in their day. It's Sam who's the black sheep of the family, not Mimi. Still, she's a very

130

smart lady, even if she does make some truly stupid public remarks. I have hope for her."

"It sounds as though winning her over is a big leap, especially given your deadline. You do have a deadline, don't you?"

"Not yet, and Mimi is the reason I don't. She's coming to dinner at my house tomorrow night, and I've invited her early for a drink, so that we can have a quiet chat. I'm not sure she'll cop to having agreed to oppose Kate Lee on everything, before she knows what everything is."

"Did you know that the Republicans have a history of that sort of obstruction, going back nearly a century?"

"I did not know that. Enlighten me."

"It's covered in Scott Berg's biography of Woodrow Wilson, which I recommend to you. Wilson went to Paris twice to head up the negotiations for what became the Treaty of Versailles, which would officially end World War One."

"That, I knew."

"Wilson's archenemy, Senator Henry Cabot Lodge Senior, held a secret meeting of important Republicans, who agreed to oppose the treaty when Wilson brought it home — no matter what the terms were. Franklin Roosevelt, who was assistant secretary of the Navy at the time, was told about it by someone who was at the meeting, but too late for him to do anything about it."

"That's fascinating."

"That's how the Republicans came to oppose the League of Nations, which Wilson had proposed in his Fourteen Points, the heart of the treaty. The League was intended to nip future wars in the bud, and Wilson said that, if the Senate did not ratify the treaty, the former combatants would be at war with each other again in twenty years."

"Which is exactly what happened."

"Now, who knows if the League could have prevented World War Two? But they would certainly have tried."

"I think we'll need to get some opinions on that from a few eminent historians. Nice to have a historical basis for our story."

"How would you like a nice, one-word title for your story?"

"Speak it!"

"CABAL."

"Perfect! It's wonderfully sinister! And appropriate in the circumstances."

They ordered dinner.

"Now," Carla said, "give me something from the inside of Kate's transition team."

Stone shrugged.

"I know you're plugged in there. I know

132

you're a member of her Kitchen Cabinet, too."

"Then you know I can't discuss anything with you that I've discussed with Kate — or anyone on her transition team."

"And I was hoping to corrupt you."

"Well," Stone said, "that's not out of the question, but you and I have to be very careful with what passes between us. We don't want to do anything that would damage your credibility as a journalist."

"You're right, of course, but it would have been fun."

"There's this, though. Kate will be president for a maximum of eight years."

"I have to wait that long to corrupt you?"

"It pains me to say it, but yes."

They had a good dinner, then he put her into a cab to her hotel. It was a nice night, and Stone walked home.

# 24

Stone was at his desk the following morning when Peter came in and accepted a chair. Stone had not seen him since the funeral. "Good morning," he said.

"Morning, Dad. The Centurion jet is coming from London this afternoon, and we're going to meet them at Teterboro tomorrow morning for the ride to L.A."

"I'll be sorry to see you all go," Stone said. "Fred will drive you to Teterboro."

"Good."

"How about a farewell dinner tonight?"

"That would be great." Peter examined a fingernail. "Dad, I need your advice about something."

"I'll give you the family rate," Stone replied. "Shoot."

"Leo Goldman has been very attentive to us since we've been at Centurion," he said. Goldman, and his father before him, were CEOs at the studio.

"That's very good."

"It has been, in lots of ways, but I'm afraid he has designs on Ben."

"Hand-on-knee designs?"

"No, employment designs. He's offered Ben the head of production job at Centurion. The current guy is retiring soon."

"Wow, that's quite a promotion for a young, independent producer with three movies under his belt."

"Ben has been spending a lot of time with Leo and the production chief, learning the operation."

"Is Ben inclined to accept?"

"He's having trouble making a decision."

"How do you feel about the situation?"

"I'd hate to lose Ben as a partner," Peter said.

"Can't he produce your films and still hold the production chief job?"

"He says he can."

"Then maybe he can. Maybe he could try the job for a year or two, and if he doesn't find it satisfying, come back to the partnership."

"Maybe, but I've got a replacement for Ben all lined up."

"Anybody I've ever heard of?"

"Teddy Fay."

Stone's eyes widened. "You're not supposed to know that name. He's Billy Burnett now."

"He sat Ben and me down a few weeks ago and told us the whole story. Said he was uncomfortable with us not knowing who we were employing. It's one hell of a story, isn't it?"

"He told you about the sealed pardon, then?"

"He did, and he's very grateful to you."

"And you think Teddy — sorry, Billy — could replace Ben?"

"Billy has been a very fast learner, and he's incredibly smart. Ben reckons he's saved us more production money than we're paying him."

"Sounds like he should have a raise."

"That will happen. So the advice I want is, what should I do? I'm emotionally attached to Ben, but I wouldn't want to stand in his way. Leo has told him that when he retires, Ben might well become the next CEO."

Stone nodded. "It sounds to me as though you don't have a decision to make."

"Oh?"

"It's Ben's decision."

"Yeah, I guess it is."

"His mother and I distributed Eduardo's estate yesterday, so Ben is now a rich man, and he can do whatever he likes."

"He told me."

"My advice is to let Ben make his decision, then, whatever it is, you find a way to live with it. Sounds like his moving up wouldn't disrupt things, what with Billy waiting in the wings. Does Billy know about all this?"

"No, I haven't mentioned it to him. But you're right, it's Ben's decision, and I'll tell him whatever he wants to do is all right with me."

"I think that's the way to go."

"One other thing bothers me, though. What if Billy's true identity becomes public? What would that do to my company?"

"To the best of my knowledge, there are only six people who know about it: you and Ben, the president, the president-elect, Billy's wife, and me. It's not in the interest of any of them for it to become known, so he's safe, and so are you. Certainly, Billy isn't going to tell anybody else."

"That's a good point," Peter said, "and I feel better about all this now. I'll talk to Ben on the way to L.A., and we'll see how it goes."

"Peter, do you think Ben has told Dino about Billy?"

"I don't know, but I'll find out."

Peter stood up and gave Stone a hug. "Thanks, Dad. You have a way of cutting through the forest to expose the trees."

Stone watched his son leave, then buzzed Joan and asked her to book a table for seven in the library at the Writing Room.

Then he contemplated the conversation he had just had with Peter. It made him feel good to have been able to give his son advice.

# 25

Dolce was in the kitchen preparing dinner when Father Frank returned from his obligatory visit to the archdiocese, clad in a black raincoat buttoned to the throat, to cover his collar, and a black hat. He was dripping wet.

"Big rain out there," he said. "What's that I smell?"

"Garlic, probably," she said, kissing him.

He hung his coat and hat on a peg by the service entrance and came back with his collar in his hand. "I'm going to change out of this wet uniform. Can I bring you a drink back?"

"I'll have some of that Irish, please."

He returned shortly with two drinks, and they clinked glasses.

"Listen, I'm going to get cabin fever if we stay cooped up here all the time."

"What's the matter? Not getting enough sex?"

He kissed her on the back of the neck. "Not nearly enough."

"We'll work on that in farthest Brooklyn," she said.

"What's in farthest Brooklyn?"

"The family," she said. "We're moving tomorrow morning."

"What sort of place?"

"We'll let that be a surprise," she said. She had another surprise for him, too; she couldn't wait to spring it.

The following morning when they were ready to go, Dolce said, "You leave the building now, make two right turns, and wait for me on the next corner. I'll pick you up."

"Shall I take my bag?"

"Yes."

"Then I'm off."

"I'll be with you in five minutes."

She got into the rented limo while the doorman put her luggage into the trunk. She had already dispatched half a dozen boxes of her own things by a messenger van. Frank was waiting where he had been told to; he put his case into the trunk and got into the rear seat.

Dolce closed the glass partition between them and the driver. "You're going to love it out there," she said.

Pietro was waiting in front of the house when they pulled up, and he took their luggage upstairs.

"Wow!" the priest said, looking around.

"Come, I'll give you the tour," Dolce said. She started with her father's study.

"This is my dream library," Frank said, scanning the titles on the shelves. "Your father and I even have a lot of the same books."

"Let me show you the art," she said, leading the way down the hall and through the living and dining rooms, with their explosion of pictures and sculpture, then she showed him the chapel. "You can pray here, and I can confess," she said, making him laugh. "Now to my favorite part of the property."

She led him out the rear doors to the garden, and they walked into the patch of woods past the mausoleum. "My father is in there," she said. Then they came out of the woods to where the old stone barn stood, on a creek leading down to the bay, the gleaming mahogany runabout in which Eduardo had enjoyed sightseeing trips in the creek and bay with Pietro at the helm bobbed at the little dock. The tide was coming in.

"The barn is not finished yet, but you can

get the idea." She pushed open the big doors at one end.

"What a wonderful space," Frank said, stepping in and looking around.

"I put in the skylights," she said. "Now the light is perfect. And I have room to do large pieces here." They skirted an area where a bucket of paint rested on a ladder and the floor was covered with a plastic drop cloth. "The painting is nearly done. They'll be back to finish on Monday." She showed him the fully equipped kitchenette. "So I won't have to go back to the main house for lunch."

"Good thinking."

She led him to a leather Chesterfield sofa that she had moved out of the master bedroom and sat him down. "We have more to think about," she said, and her heart was pounding.

"What's on your mind?" Frank asked. He took on a professional mien.

"Now don't get all priestly with me. This is a conversation between a man and a woman."

Frank laughed. "I guess I'm not accustomed to that conversation," he said.

"Have you enjoyed your time here, Frank?"

"Have I ever! You lead the most wonderful life, and I've been lucky to share a little of it."

"How would you like to share it all?" she asked, stroking his cheek.

"It's a lovely idea, but I don't see how it's possible," he replied. "I can't commute from the Vatican."

"It's not only possible, it's easy," she said. "All you have to do is say yes. I'll do the rest."

"You mean I should go back, resign, and move in with you?"

"You don't even have to go back," she said. "You can mail them your resignation." She kissed him.

"That is an overwhelming thought," Frank said.

"We'll have the Park Avenue apartment, and this estate — all ours. And whatever else we might want in the world."

"What would I do with my time?"

"You're a psychiatrist — open a practice. I'll set you up with an office in a good building. I expect there's a good trade to be had in lapsed Catholics and their resulting guilt."

He laughed. "They're thick on the ground, all right, but there's something you don't understand."

"What's that, my darling?"

"I'm a priest. Not just by education and

title — it's what I am, through and through, and I can't do that and be with you all the time, too."

"You can go on being a priest," she said. "I'd rather like that."

"How on earth could I continue as a priest and simultaneously be with you?"

"Become an Episcopalian. They would welcome you. I'll buy you a good church. They'll deal just like anybody else. A contribution to whatever they like, and you get your pick of churches."

"Sweetheart, I'm a *Roman Catholic* priest. If I couldn't be that, I'd slowly die."

Dolce began to feel her blood getting warm, and her face became pink. She felt herself becoming desperate. "You'd reject me, just like that?" She snapped her fingers.

"Don't you think I've dreamed about doing just what you suggest? I've thought of it again and again, but the Church is there, tugging at my sleeve. Always and forever. That is my only destiny."

"I see," Dolce said, rising. She walked into the kitchenette and got a bottle of water from the fridge, then she took a boning knife from the wooden block that held the implements and held it, blade up her sleeve. "Come here, Frank," she said. "There's something I want to show you." She set

144

down the water, because her hand was trembling.

He got up and came toward her; they met in the center of the room. She took his arm and maneuvered him onto the plastic drop cloth.

"What do you want to show me?" Frank asked.

"Only, this," she said, drawing back the knife and swinging it at him in a wide arc. The razor-sharp blade found its mark, leaving a six-inch slit that included both the carotid artery and the jugular vein.

Frank clutched at his throat, trying to speak, but making only a gurgling noise. Blood poured down his chest.

She took his arm and tugged. "This way a little bit," she said. "We don't want to make a mess, do we?"

Frank's knees buckled and he sank onto the plastic drop cloth. At first, a pool of blood spread, but then it stopped.

"I'll just get some tape," Dolce said. She came back with a thick roll of masking tape and had a good look at him. He was already gone. Then she went to work.

An hour later, after a rest to calm herself, Dolce walked back to the main house and rang for Pietro.

The man appeared quickly. "Yes, ma'am?"

"Pietro," Dolce said, "my father always told me that you were a man who could be relied upon in any situation."

"I am proud that he thought so," Pietro replied. "I was at his beck and call, as I now am at yours. My duty is anything you should require."

"I have a job for you," she said, and she explained.

Pietro made a little bow. "It shall be done," he said.

"And don't forget his luggage, upstairs."

She poured herself a drink, avoiding the Irish whiskey, and sat down, taking deep breaths, allowing her heart and respiration to return to normal.

# 26

Stone, Peter and Hattie, Ben and Tessa, and Dino and Viv gathered in the rear library room of the Writing Room for dinner. It occurred to him that he was the only stag there; he wished Ann could be there, too. It also came to him that, one day, one of these dinners would be their last together. He hoped that would not be for a long time.

They ordered drinks and dinner, and Stone found an excellent Cabernet on the wine list and ordered two bottles.

Then Stone heard a knife rapping on a glass and the table became quiet.

Peter spoke up. "Ben has an announcement to make," he said. "The floor is yours, partner."

"Thanks, Peter," Ben said, keeping his seat. "Peter and I have been having some serious conversations lately, and with his agreement, I've made an important decision in my life."

Stone noticed that Dino seemed to have no idea what was coming.

"Peter and I have made a wonderful team, and we will continue to collaborate. However, Centurion Studios has offered me the job of head of production for the whole studio, and I just can't resist it. I'll be moving to an office in the executive building, but I'll keep my office at our building, too. This is all effective next week." He stopped and looked around.

It was quiet for a moment, then everybody cheered and clapped. Dino walked over, stood him up, and hugged him. "Now you're going to be making more money than your old man," he said, pounding Ben on his back.

"Dad," Ben said, "I hate to break this to you, but I've been making more money than you since I left Yale."

Everybody laughed, no one harder than Dino.

Dino's phone vibrated. He picked up his drink, stepped away from the table, and entered into earnest conversation.

"The NYPD never closes," Viv said.

Dino came back and sat down with his drink. He didn't say anything.

"Come on, Dino," Stone said, "let us be the first to hear the news."

148

"What news?" Dino asked.

"The news you just got on the phone."

"Oh, *that news.*"

"Come on, Dad, give!" Ben said.

"It's not going to go very well with the osso buco."

"We'll live."

"All right: a couple of hours ago a trawler in Jamaica Bay pulled in the trawl and found, in addition to many examples of marine life, a severed head in a weighted plastic bag. Quite fresh, too."

"Ugh," Tessa said, and made a face.

"I warned you, but my friend and my son just had to know."

"Whose head was it?" Hattie asked.

"The full resources of the NYPD are now directed at answering that question," Dino replied. "How soon we know will depend on whether the gentleman has a DNA record or dental records on file somewhere."

"I guess there are no fingerprints," Ben said drily.

Groans from all present.

Dinner arrived, Stone tasted and poured the wine, and they all dug into dinner.

They had just finished the dessert wine and were on coffee when Dino got another call. As before, he stepped away from the table to answer it. He talked for five minutes or so, then returned and sat down. "I can now answer your question, Hattie," he said.

"Oh, please. Is it anybody we know?"

"No," Dino said. "Sorry to disappoint. The head belongs to an Irishman."

"You can get DNA records from Ireland on such short notice?" Peter asked.

"Yes, but in this case, not from Ireland, but from the Vatican, which keeps those records on all its employees, including the Pope. The Irishman was a priest. His name is Father Frank Donovan, and he was executive assistant to the head of the Vatican Bank, Cardinal Penzi."

"A priest?" somebody asked.

"A priest and a banker."

"There's a history of suicide connected to the Vatican Bank, isn't there?" Ben asked.

"Somehow, I don't think this one was a suicide," Dino replied, and everybody laughed again.

"I thought the Vatican Bank had been cleaned out of executives and was under new management," Stone said.

"This guy was new management," Dino replied.

"Well," Hattie said, "if I may paraphrase Ronald Reagan, where's the rest of him?"

"Arrangements are being made now to drag the bay, starting at first light tomorrow," Dino said. "We'll reassemble him, if we can."

Somebody changed the subject and the mood lightened again.

# 27

Stone got himself out of bed in time to have breakfast in the kitchen with the kids before they left for the airport.

"So what's next for you, Peter? Got a picture in mind?"

"I have a good script, but the new head of production is going to have to approve it before we start casting," Peter said.

"All right, all right," Ben said, throwing up his hands. "Your script and your budget are approved. I've already read it, and I did the budget."

"I hope he's this easy to work with in the future," Peter said.

Stone walked them out to the car, where Fred waited. "The luggage is aboard," Fred said. "These young people travel light, they do."

Stone hugged everybody and put them into the car; he waved them off and went back to the front door. He paused there to look at a man on the other side of the street who seemed to be watching him or his house. He wore a black overcoat and a gray felt hat, and a muffler that partially obscured his face. Apparently aware that he had been noticed, the man began walking quickly toward Third Avenue. Stone watched him hail a cab at the corner and drive away. Who, he asked himself, would be watching him or having him watched? He couldn't come up with an answer.

Stone went back upstairs, showered, shaved, then dressed and went down to his office. Joan was putting some mail on his desk. "Did you notice someone watching the house from across the street earlier?" Stone asked.

"Nope. Has some husband put a detective on you?"

"The women I see don't have husbands," Stone said.

"A distraught old flame, then?"

"My old flames are never distraught, they're relieved."

"Except for one," she said, then left the room.

It took Stone a moment to get it. "She's out of the picture!" he called as she turned into her office.

Joan stuck her head out. "Funny, I thought

153

she was back *in* the picture." She dis-appeared again.

Stone found the thought unsettling. He hoped to God that the whole thing with Dolce wasn't starting over.

Dolce slept in until she was awakened by Pietro's rap on the door. "Come in!"

The butler opened the door and stuck in his head. "A dozen crates have been delivered," he said. "Where would you like them put?"

"In the new studio, please, and ask them to unpack them very carefully and dispose of the crates."

"Yes, madam. By the way, the task you asked me to perform has been completed." Pietro vanished.

Dolce ordered her breakfast and showered while she waited for it. She felt curiously lighthearted at the absence of Frank Donovan; he hadn't been good enough for her, and she had disposed of him, and that was that. Breakfast came, and she didn't give Frank another thought.

She thought about Stone Barrington, though. She had liked being Mrs. Barrington, while it lasted. Many of her memories of that time were cloudy, or simply absent. She knew she had done some bad things, but in retrospect, they didn't seem all that bad.

Later that morning she had Pietro bring a ladder to the old barn, and she began hanging pictures on the wall opposite the one where the painters were at work.

"We found some spots of red paint on the floor, ma'am," one of them said to her. "Funny, we aren't using any red paint, but we cleaned it up. It didn't leave a stain."

"Thank you," Dolce said, and returned to her work.

Stone came back from lunch and found a note from Dino. He returned the call.

"Hey," Dino said.

"Sounds like you're in the car."

"I'm headed up to the archdiocese," Dino said. "Our divers found most of the rest of Father Donovan."

"How much is most?"

"Both legs, the torso, and the right arm. I called 'em off. I don't see any reason to pay overtime for a left arm, when we've got all we need."

"I hope you'll put that a bit more tactfully to the cardinal."

"Oh, I will be the soul of tact when I speak to His Grace."

"Did you get a cause of death?"

155

"The ME says his throat was cut before the head was severed. Seems pretty straight-forward. Now I've got to go unload the remains on the archdiocese."

"That would seem the simplest way to get rid of them."

"I hope they don't insist on finding the other arm," Dino said. "Did the kids get off okay this morning?"

"Right on schedule."

"Imagine a son of mine, head of produc-tion at a Hollywood studio!"

"Peter's a little upset about that, but he doesn't want to show it. He's fortunate in having Billy Burnett to take up the slack." Stone waited for Dino to mention Teddy Fay, but he didn't.

"Gotta dump you for the cardinal," Dino said. "Talk to you later."

# 28

Stone was on the phone with a client that afternoon when Joan came and stuck her head in. "Just a minute," he said, then covered the phone. "What is it, Joan?"

"There's a man out here who insists on seeing you, but he won't give his name."

"Describe him."

"Five-eight or -nine, a hundred and forty, late thirties, early forties. Black overcoat."

It sounded like the man watching from across the street. "Tell him I'm on a phone call and to wait."

"He looks as though he might bolt at any minute."

"If he bolts, he bolts." Stone went back to his call. It took another ten minutes to ease his client's mind, then he hung up and buzzed Joan.

"Send him in."

"He bolted."

"Check outside and see if he's hanging

around."

He waited while she looked, then he heard the chime that meant the front door was open, and Joan said, "Please go right in there."

The man appeared in the doorway, holding his hat and looking nervous.

Stone had never seen him, but he thought he knew who he was. "Come in, Congressman, and have a seat."

Joan appeared behind the man. "May I take your coat?"

He jumped, then reluctantly gave up his coat and hat and sat in the chair that Stone indicated.

"Good morning," Evan Hills said.

"Good morning. Why didn't you come in earlier?"

"You seemed to be involved with your family. I didn't want to intrude."

"One of the young men is my son, the others are his friends."

"Ah."

"What can I do for you, Congressman?"

"That's difficult to say."

"Try. And by the way, I admire what you're doing."

Hills's shoulders slumped. "I just want out."

"You can do that, if it's really what you

want. The *Times* already has your statement, and they won't reveal your identity."

"I mean out of everything."

Stone began to realize what he was dealing with. "I'd like to help," he said. "What can I do to help?"

"I don't seem to have any alternatives."

"There are always alternatives, it's just that sometimes none of them seem attractive. It seems to me you have at least three choices: One, you can continue as you are, and when your political colleagues suspect you, deny everything. The only evidence that you might be involved is your presence at that meeting, and that applies equally to the other two dozen people who were there. Two, you can resign from Congress and go home to Philadelphia, or wherever else in the world you might like to go, blaming ill health. Three, you can make a public statement, associate yourself with the *Times* piece, and resign from your party, become an independent or a Democrat."

"You're right, none of those alternatives is very attractive."

"Tell me, in the best of all possible worlds, what would you like to be doing a year from now?"

Hills sat and thought. "I'd like to have a

law practice in some small town in Pennsylvania."

"Is that within your means?"

"Yes, I'm quite well off."

"Then why don't you do just that?"

"They'll find me," he said. "They'll hunt me down and . . ."

Stone waited for him to continue, but he didn't.

"Let me pose another question, then: During the next year, what is the worst thing that could happen to you?"

"I'd be hounded out of Congress and the party, most of the people I think of as my friends wouldn't ever speak to me again, I'd be thrown out of my old law firm. Or, it might even be worse."

"All of those things sound like a predicate for your doing what you want to do, except the last one. What would be worse?"

"I might be dead."

"Are you ill?"

"No, I'm very fit."

"Do you suspect someone of wanting you dead?"

"Half the people I know — if they knew what I'd done."

"What you've done is courageous and good," Stone said. "Has it occurred to you that, if it became known, you would gain many new friends?"

"You mean Democrats?"

"I mean people who will admire what you've done. Many of them might be Republicans who don't like what's happening to their party."

"I'm not really cut out for being a rebel."

"The rebelling is already behind you. You just have to figure out what you want and go do it."

"They won't let me do that."

"Who are 'they'?"

"Powerful people who don't show their faces to the world."

"For every one of them who wants to destroy you, there'll be others who want to help."

"I wish I could believe that."

"If you're concerned for your safety, I can arrange protection. If you want to disappear, I own the house next door, and there's a comfortable guest apartment that you're welcome to, for as long as it takes."

Hills, who had been staring disconsolately into the middle distance, suddenly focused, maybe even brightened a bit. "You'd do that for me?"

"I would."

"All right," he said, standing up. "I have to make some arrangements first and get my things from my hotel."

"My advice is not to tell anyone where you are, at least for a couple of days," Stone said. "And then think carefully about who you tell."

"There's only one person," Hills said.

Stone buzzed for Joan, and she came in. "Joan, this is Mr. Hills. He's going to be staying next door for a while. Will you ask Helene to make sure the apartment is ready for him?"

"Of course," Joan said.

"How long before you'll be back?" Stone asked.

"An hour at the most," Hills said.

"We'll look forward to seeing you. Enter through the office door, and Joan will take you next door."

Hills offered his hand, the first time he had done so, and Stone shook it.

"One other thing," Hills said.

"Yes?"

"I made a recording of the meeting."

"Good. You may need it."

"Thank you so much, Mr. Barrington." Hills put on his coat and hat and left, looking relieved.

Hills walked up to Third Avenue and looked for a cab. His cell phone buzzed, and he checked the caller ID. "Hello?"

"Are you all right?"

"I'm fine. I'm going to stay in New York for a while. Got a pencil?"

"Yep."

Hills gave him the address. "You can always reach me on my cell."

"Let me give you some advice. Get one of those prepaid throwaway cell phones from an electronics shop, and don't give the number to anyone but me."

"I'll do that right now," Hills said. He hung up and walked up Third Avenue, looking for a place to buy the phone.

# 29

Stone tidied his desk, then walked into Joan's office. "Did the congressman come back?"

"Is that what he is? No, he didn't."

Stone looked at his watch. "He said he'd be back inside an hour. It's been nearly two."

"What can I tell you?"

"Well, show him to the suite when he returns. I'm going upstairs for a while, then to dinner with Dino at Clarke's." Stone went up to his study, poured himself a drink, and settled in to watch the news. The anchorwoman finished a report, then turned to another camera. "This just in: there's been a hit-and-run at the corner of Park Avenue and Fifty-seventh Street, and a man is dead. Don Kerr is at the scene."

The live shot came up. "Deborah, the ambulance has just taken the man's body away, and an officer told me that there was identification in his pockets, but they're not releasing the name pending notification of next of kin. I have with me a gentleman who saw it happen." He stuck the microphone in a man's face.

"Yeah, I saw it. The guy was jaywalking, but there was no excuse to hit him. It could have been avoided."

"What kind of car was it?"

"It was black — an SUV, I think."

"Did you see the license plate?"

"Just a glimpse. It wasn't a New York plate."

"Have the police interviewed you?"

"Yeah, I talked to two detectives."

Kerr turned back to the camera. "That's it, Deborah, until we get an ID on the victim."

Stone tuned out what Deborah was saying now. He had an awful feeling that he didn't want to give in to. He called Dino.

"Hey," Dino said.

"Hey. Do you keep track of hit-and-runs?"

"Not personally, but we get a lot of them."

"There was one this afternoon at Fifty-seventh and Park, and the TV said he had ID on him. Can you find out his name?"

"Call you right back."

Stone switched to MSNBC and the Chris Matthews show, then he tugged at his drink

165

and worried. Ten minutes passed, and the phone rang.

"Yes?"

"The guy's ID says he was a U.S. congressman named Evan Hills."

"Oh, shit."

"Did you know him?"

"Barely."

"Dinner tonight? I'm batching it."

"Clarke's at seven-thirty?"

"You're on." Dino hung up.

Stone called Carla Fontana. "I've got bad news," he said to her.

"What?"

"Evan Hills is dead."

"Oh, God."

"Hit-and-run at Park and Fifty-seventh Street."

"In New York?"

"Right. He came to see me earlier this afternoon."

"What sort of frame of mind was he in?"

"Despondent, I'd say."

"I think he was getting shaky."

"He told me he wanted out, and he didn't mean the story."

"Are you saying he was suicidal?"

"I think maybe so. I offered him an apartment in the house I own next door, and he accepted. He was going back to his hotel to get his luggage. The local news said he was jaywalking, but a witness said the accident was avoidable. It was a black SUV with an out-of-state tag. His identity hasn't been made public yet. I found out from a friend at the NYPD."

"You think he was murdered?"

"I think he was afraid he was going to be murdered, but it's a toss-up. It could have been just an accident. We get a lot of hit-and-runs in the city."

"Well, at least we have his statement."

"You may have more than that."

"What do you mean?"

"He told me he had a recording of the meeting, and that the voices were clearly distinguishable."

"Did you hear it?"

"No. He may not have had it on him."

"Can your friend at the NYPD find out if the police found it?"

"Maybe. I'll call him."

"I'll call our New York city desk and get them on it."

He looked at his watch. "I've got a dinner date with my friend. I'll let you know what he says." He hung up, got his coat, and headed for P.J. Clarke's.

# 30

The bar at Clarke's was jammed, and Stone practically had to elbow his way through the career women and metrosexuals. Dino wasn't there yet, but the headwaiter knew him and gave him a fairly quiet table, where he ordered a drink.

Stone remembered that Hills had said he had only one friend he trusted, and he wondered who the friend was — maybe the man who owned the antiques shop where Carla had met with Hills. He called Carla.

"Anything new?" she asked.

"Nothing yet on the recording, but Hills told me there was only one person he would tell where he was, and I think it could be the man who owns the antiques shop. Why don't you talk to him? He probably hasn't heard about the event yet."

"I'll do that right now."

"I'll be on my cell."

Dino walked in, hung up his coat, and sat

down. His scotch magically appeared. "What a day!" He raised his glass and drank.

"Dino, have you released the congressman's name to the media yet?"

"Nah, not until tomorrow. We're having trouble finding a next of kin. His father's phone is immediately answered by a machine, and he hasn't returned our calls."

"There are some things I'd better tell you," Stone said. He gave Dino a blow-by-blow of the meeting, the phone call he'd received from Hills, and his contact with Carla Fontana.

"Isn't she the one who interviewed you in Paris?"

"Right. She's put together a big story on the meeting, and she has a statement from Hills. What she didn't know is that Hills had a recording of the meeting. He told me this afternoon."

"You saw him?"

"He came to my office and seemed very worried. He thought his life was in danger. I offered him the apartment next door, and he left to get his luggage. He didn't come back. And, Dino, he was talking about checking out."

"So you think he could have picked a car and just walked in front of it?"

"I think it's about as much a possibility as

someone murdering him. That part is far-fetched. I think he was just being paranoid."

"Did you hear the recording?"

"No."

"Did he say how he recorded it?"

"No, but an iPhone would do it."

Dino got out his cell phone and made a call. "It's Bacchetti," he said. "Have you got the hit-and-run victim's belongings?" He listened for a bit. "Did he have an iPhone or some other recording device on him? Bring it to me at Clarke's, and tell your people to canvass the neighborhood, and when you find it, search his room for a recording device and if you find it, bring it to me." He hung up. "He had an iPhone, and it's on its way, but they haven't found his hotel room yet. They're canvassing every place in the neighborhood."

They ordered dinner, and by the time they had finished their first course, a detective, Garbanza, was at their table. Dino introduced him to Stone.

"There's a recording on the phone," the detective said. "Some sort of political meeting."

"Can I have the phone?" Stone asked.

"Of course not," Dino said. "It's evidence."

"I just want to record his recording. I

won't mess it up."

Dino nodded and Garbanza opened his briefcase, took the phone from a plastic evidence bag, found a cable and plugged it into Stone's iPhone. "I'll sync it for you." He selected the recording and pressed a button. Dinner came, and they began to eat. The syncing ran for half an hour. Garbanza unhooked the phones and returned Stone's. "If that's who I think it is on the recording, it's hot stuff," he said.

"The *Times* already has Hills's statement about the meeting. The recording will back up his account," Stone said.

"If you haven't reached a next of kin by nine tomorrow morning, release Hills's name to the media," Dino said, "but don't say anything about the recording, and I want that phone secured, and I mean *secured* until further notice. Got it?"

"Got it," Garbanza said.

"Not a word to anybody, not even your partner."

"Got it." The detective put the phone back into the bag, put the bag into his briefcase, and left.

Stone's phone rang. "Hello?"

"It's Carla."

"Did you talk to him?"

"Yes, and he's a mixture of broken up and

mad as hell. Hills called him this afternoon and gave him your address. The man's name is Bruce Willard. He was going to meet Hills in New York on Sunday."

"Did he say where Hills was staying?"

"At the Lowell, Sixty-third and Madison. It was Hills's regular place in the city."

"Hang on." Stone covered the phone. "Hills was staying at the Lowell."

"That's in my block."

"I know."

Dino got on his phone and Stone went back to his. "The recording was on Hills's iPhone," he said, "and it's been copied to mine. The police have sequestered the phone and it won't be mentioned when they release Hills's name to the press tomorrow morning. They haven't been able to reach his father."

"He's reclusive, I hear. I'll see if I know someone who can reach him. Can I send someone to where you are to pick up the recording?"

"Let's take care of that tomorrow. I'll transfer it to tape and FedEx it to you."

"All right. Good night."

Stone hung up. "She's going to try to reach Hills's father. Apparently he's something of a recluse."

They finished dinner, then Dino dropped off Stone at home.

## 31

Stone had just gotten into bed when his phone rang. He picked up the bedside handset. "Hello?"

"Mr. Barrington? You don't know me. My name is Bruce Willard. Evan Hills gave me your number this afternoon."

"I know who you are, Mr. Willard. Evan mentioned you."

"I called the New York police and tried to find out what happened to him, but they wouldn't talk to me, because I wasn't a family member. Can you tell me what happened?"

Stone brought Willard up to date on the hit-and-run and subsequent events.

"Do you know what's on the recording?"

"I haven't listened to it yet, but I believe it was made at the meeting that Evan has been talking to Carla Fontana about."

"Nothing else?"

"Not that I know of."

"What will be done with the recording?"

"It will go to Carla, at the *Times.*"

"I'm supposed to have lunch with her tomorrow."

"She'll have the recording by that time."

"I suppose Evan told you he was worried about those people coming after him."

"He did tell me that, and I tried to ease his mind. That kind of thing happens only in the movies. American politicians don't actually kill each other, though I'm sure there are times when they'd like to."

"I wouldn't be too sure about that," Willard said.

"Did Evan give you any details of exactly whom he was afraid of?"

"No, he was vague, he just referred to 'them.' "

"A witness said on TV that Evan was jaywalking, so it could be an accident, and the driver just panicked. Often in these cases the driver will talk to the police later."

"There was one name that Evan mentioned. He works at some lobbying firm in Washington, for several right-wing groups. His name is Creed Harker . . ." He spelled the name. "Evan said his specialty was dirty work."

"Did he say what kind of dirty work?"

"Tampering with elections, character

smears, taking pictures in bedrooms — creepy stuff. Evan thought he'd do anything he was paid to do."

"Have you ever met him?"

"Evan once pointed him out to me in the lobby of the Four Seasons Hotel in Georgetown: very tall, wiry, bald as an egg, no eyebrows. He looks like a space alien in a bad movie."

"Did Evan say anything else about him?"

"Just that he wouldn't like to meet him in a dark alley."

"Well, Mr. Willard, talk to Carla and keep reading the *Times*. They're going to be writing a lot about this."

"All right, Mr. Barrington. Thank you for your time."

"And, Mr. Willard, I'm very sorry for your loss. He was a nice man."

"He was a lot more than that, Mr. Barrington, but thank you for the sentiment." Willard hung up.

Stone felt sorry for the man.

The following morning when Stone went down to his office, he found a thick envelope on his desk. Joan came in with some phone messages.

"Where'd this come from?" he asked, holding up the envelope.

"It was on the hall table in the waiting

176

area," she said. "Maybe Mr. Hills left it."

Stone slit open the envelope and took out several pages. There was a letter on fine stationery, handwritten.

Dear Mr. Barrington,

There's no one I can trust in Washington with this, so I'm turning to you. I hereby appoint you as my sole attorney and legal adviser and as executor of my estate. I enclose the original of my will, recently drawn and witnessed by three of the staff at the Georgetown Four Seasons Hotel, where I frequently lunch and dine.

This is not a spur-of-the-moment decision. I've thoroughly checked you out, and I'm very satisfied with what I've learned about you. My will is as simple and clear as I know how to make it, and I'm a pretty good lawyer myself.

I enclose a copy of the recording I told you about and a check for a retainer. You may bill me at the above address for any further charges. Thank you for your consideration in this matter.

Cordially,
Evan Hills

There was a mini-cassette enclosed and a

check for $25,000, drawn on a Georgetown bank.

Stone read the will and the attached financial statement. He had left a dozen or so bequests to employees, congressional staff members, and arts organizations, and the remainder of his assets were left to Bruce Willard, of a Pennsylvania Avenue address in Georgetown.

Hills's property included a house in Philadelphia, another in Bucks County, Pennsylvania, a house in Georgetown, and three investment accounts showing cash and securities in excess of twenty million dollars. He had no debts older than thirty days, and the will was dated two days before.

Joan was still standing in the door. "Anything?"

"We have a new client," he said, handing her everything but the mini-cassette. "He died yesterday, so start a file." He held up the mini-cassette. "Duplicate this, and FedEx one of the copies to Carla Fontana, at the *New York Times* Washington bureau."

"Got it," Joan said, and left his office.

## 32

Stone was tidying up his desk at the end of the day when he heard the doorbell ring, and Joan buzzed him.

"There's a Mr. Bruce Willard to see you," she said. "He says you know him."

Stone sat back down. "Send him in," he said.

A solidly built man of around six feet, with salt-and-pepper, closely cropped hair, appeared in the doorway, shucking off a sheepskin coat for Joan to take.

"Come in, Mr. Willard," Stone said, catching a glimpse of hardware under the man's tweed jacket. "Have a seat, and please give me the handgun you're wearing. We don't permit weapons in our offices, except those of law enforcement officers."

Willard produced a 9mm Beretta, of the type used as a military sidearm, and handed it to Stone across his desk. Stone popped the magazine and ejected the round in the chamber onto his desktop, then he opened the small safe in his desk and secured the weapon. Finally, he offered his hand to Willard, who shook it with an iron grip. "How do you do?"

"Not very well," Willard said. "I'm being followed."

"By whom? Any ideas?"

"Some of them are in black SUVs," he replied. "As paranoid as that may sound."

"It doesn't sound all that paranoid, when you consider that Evan Hills was run down by a black SUV. When did this start?"

"I first noticed them around noon, when I left my place of business to have lunch at the Four Seasons Georgetown with Carla Fontana. They were still around when I left the hotel, and I thought I spotted a couple of guys on foot."

"What did they look like?"

"Like me," Willard said. "Ex–Special Forces, very fit."

"Where did you serve?"

"Two tours each, in Iraq and Afghanistan, and other places I can't tell you about."

"Your Beretta seemed well-used."

"You could say that. I'm pretty well-used, myself."

"What brings you to New York?"

"I don't feel safe in D.C.," Willard said.

"You offered Evan refuge here — I hoped you might do the same for me."

"Of course," Stone said. He buzzed Joan and asked her to get the apartment next door ready.

"It's been ready since yesterday," she said.

"And please make a copy of those documents I gave you earlier and bring it to me." Stone put the phone down. "You have an antiques shop on Pennsylvania Avenue in Georgetown, is that right?"

"Yes. It's where I met Evan. He came in several times as a customer and we became friends. That was before he was elected to Congress."

"Do you live over the shop?"

"Yes, why do you ask?"

"I was sent a document that listed your address as what sounded like the shop."

"I have a duplex apartment upstairs and another that I rent."

"Let me explain about the weapon," Stone said. "New York City has a very tough weapons law, and it's almost impossible for an ordinary citizen to get a carry permit, unless he can prove he's routinely transporting large amounts of cash or jewelry. Possession is a serious matter and carries a prison sentence. The police don't look kindly upon visitors to the city who arrive armed."

"I understand. Thank you for telling me."

"Did you fly here?"

"No, I rented a car and returned it here. I thought I might be less likely to be followed, and I didn't notice anyone on my tail."

"Do you mind if I ask you some questions about Evan — and you?"

"Not at all."

"How long ago did you meet?"

"About three years ago."

"When did you become more than just friends?"

"About three months after we met. Evan was very paranoid about being gay. He had worked in politics for years and had given large donations to his party, but he knew he'd be ostracized if he came out or was discovered. He wouldn't visit me more than once a week, and when he did, he always bought some object or picture and left carrying it. His house is full of things he bought from me, and they were, without exception, the finest pieces I had to offer. He was my best customer — our relationship apart — and his taste was superb."

Joan came in with the copies Stone had asked for.

Stone handed the letter from Hills to

Willard. "He left this here on his visit yesterday."

Willard read the letter carefully, then read it again.

Stone handed him the will. "And this."

Willard read it and began to cry.

Stone was taken aback; Willard didn't look like the sort of man who would allow himself to be seen weeping. He pushed a box of tissues across the desk, and Willard took a handful, dabbed at his face, and blew his nose noisily.

"I'm sorry for my conduct," he said.

"You've nothing to be sorry for," Stone replied.

"You see, Evan knew that the income from the shop and the apartment kept me operating pretty close to the line. All I have beyond that is my disability pension from the military." He held up the will. "This changes everything for me."

"I expect it does," Stone said, handing him Hills's financial statement.

Willard read it and began to weep again.

# 33

Stone was in his study watching the news when Joan came in. "Is Mr. Willard all settled in?"

"Yes. Helene is making him some dinner. What a very nice man he is!"

"He charmed you pretty quickly, didn't he?"

"He certainly did. He's also very handsome."

"I wouldn't let that go to your head."

"Oh, I know he's gay. I could tell, but women love gay men."

"Because they're harmless?"

"Because, in my experience, they're sympathetic and understanding," she said. "He's quite broken up over his loss, you know."

"I'm aware of that."

"I hope you were sympathetic."

"Of course I was. I offered my condolences and gave him tissues."

"Did you really?"

"And shelter from his enemies."

"Who are his enemies?"

"That has not yet been determined."

"Has it been determined whether his enemies are real or imagined?"

"If Evan Hills was run down deliberately, he has enemies. If he wasn't, he may still have enemies, real ones."

There was a tap at the door, and Stone looked up to see Bruce Willard standing there.

"Come in, Bruce. May I call you that?"

"Of course."

"And I'm Stone. Would you like a drink?"

"I could use one." Willard took a seat on the sofa.

"Joan? As long as you're here?"

"I'll drink some of that awful whiskey you like so much."

Stone went to the bar. "One Knob Creek, coming up. Bruce?"

"The same, please, rocks."

Stone poured and distributed the drinks.

"Sit down, Joan."

She sat, taking the other end of the sofa from where Willard sat.

"I understand you have an antiques shop, Bruce," she said.

"Yes, I do."

"Do you have a specialty?"

"It's pretty eclectic. I do very well with Georgian silver."

"I love Georgian silver."

Maybe I should leave the two of them alone, Stone thought. The phone rang. "Stone Barrington."

"It's Carla."

"Hi, there."

"I had a very nice lunch with Bruce Willard."

"So I hear."

"You talked to him?"

"We're having a drink at my house now."

"Do you mind if I join you?"

"We'd be delighted. Where are you?"

"In a cab from the airport."

"Then come straight here. We'll have dinner here, too."

"See you in twenty." She hung up.

"That was Carla. She's coming here. Why don't we all have dinner?"

"Thank you," Willard said.

"Joan, will you call Helene and tell her we'll be four? And would you please bring me that tape I was going to send to Carla?"

Joan went to the phone on the desk and called downstairs. "Helene wants to know what you'd like."

"Something Greek," Stone said.

"Something Greek," Joan said into the phone. "Got it." She hung up. "Forty-five minutes — she was already halfway there." Joan left the room and came back with the tape.

Carla arrived in time for a second round. "Fancy meeting you here," she said to Bruce, accepting a martini from Stone.

"Small world," he replied.

"I have news," Carla said. "We're running in the Sunday paper, and it's a spread in Section A."

"Great," Stone said.

"I hope so," Bruce replied.

Stone gave Carla the tape. "Here it is."

"Good, now we can publish quotes. There's still time to get some in, we don't close until tomorrow night."

"I suppose I should be relieved," Bruce sighed.

"Look at it this way, Bruce," Stone said. "After the story runs, no one will be trying to stop you from saying whatever you were going to say. No one will feel any need to harm you."

"Then it's a pity it didn't run sooner," Bruce said. "Evan might still be alive."

# 34

They had finished dinner and were on coffee and brandy when Carla's cell phone went off, and she excused herself from the table.

"There must be some problem with publication," Bruce said.

Carla returned. "The publisher got a call from a billionaire fund-raiser, he wouldn't say who, trying to talk him out of publishing our piece. Somebody has talked about our pub date."

"Oh, God," Bruce said, "this is never going to end."

"He told the man in no uncertain terms that he was publishing," she said, "and they're sending a messenger over here for the tape. Stop worrying, Bruce, my paper doesn't get pushed around."

"Would this be the same billionaire who hosted the infamous meeting?" Stone asked.

"That's my supposition," she said. "Tomorrow, I'll ask for permission to publish the name of the caller, and I'm likely to get it."

Bruce polished off his brandy and set his glass down. "If you'll excuse me, it's been a long day, and I'm going to turn in."

"Tomorrow morning, dial three on the phone and ask Helene for breakfast."

"Thank you," he said, rising, "and good night to you all."

The phone buzzed, and Stone picked it up. "Yes? Someone will be right there." He hung up. "Carla, that's your messenger at the door."

Carla grabbed her purse and went upstairs.

"I think that's my cue to go home," Joan said.

"Sleep well."

"I always do. A clear conscience will do that for you." She left the table and went upstairs.

Stone followed her and ran into Carla.

"That's done," she said. "May I use your phone? I forgot to call my usual hotel."

"This is practically a hotel," Stone said. "Take a guest room." Before she could protest, he got her bag from the study and led her to the elevator, then he installed her in a bedroom.

189

"I'm just down the hall, if you need anything," he said. "And dial three for breakfast."

"Thank you, Stone." She kissed him on the cheek, brushing the corner of his mouth.

"There are robes in the closet," he said. "Good night."

"Good night."

He closed the door behind him and walked down the hall to the master suite. He undressed, got into bed, and turned on the eleven o'clock news. A couple of reports in, a photograph of a black SUV with a smashed front fender came onto the screen.

"A vehicle police said was involved in a Manhattan hit-and-run yesterday has been found parked on a public street in Newark, New Jersey," the anchorwoman said. "It was registered to a Washington, D.C., security firm called Integral Security and was reported stolen by that firm last night. Police sources tell us it had been wiped clean of fingerprints."

Stone switched off the TV and fell asleep.

Stone was sleeping soundly on his side when a fingernail ran down his spine, causing him to jump.

"I'd say I was sorry to wake you, but I'm not," Carla said.

Stone turned over, and she came into his

arms, naked.

"You can ask me to leave, and I will," she said. "But I hope you won't."

Stone began to feel receptive. "As a matter of policy," he said, "I never kick a beautiful, naked woman out of bed."

"I'm glad I qualify."

"On both counts."

Another hour passed before they fell asleep.

When Stone awoke he could hear the shower running. He called Helene and ordered breakfast, then turned on *Morning Joe.* Shortly, Carla appeared in a guest robe, her hair wet. She climbed into bed, and he used the remote to sit them up.

"Breakfast is on the way," he said.

"Do I have time to dry my hair?"

"If it doesn't take long."

She ran back to the bathroom, and he heard the dryer running. By the time she came back, the tray was out of the dumbwaiter and on the bed between them.

"It's scrambled eggs with cheese, and applewood smoked bacon," he said. "I hope it's not too much."

"Are you kidding? I'm starved!" She tossed aside the cover and dug in.

Somebody on *Morning Joe* was talking. "There's a rumor that the *New York Times*

191

is running a major investigative piece on Sunday that may be tied to the death of Congressman Evan Hills, Republican of Pennsylvania."

Carla sat up straight. "How can they possibly know that?" she asked. "This is getting annoying."

"He said it's a rumor," Stone pointed out.

"Anybody heard anything?" the journalist asked.

"Only what you've heard," somebody said.

"Then I guess we'll have to wait for the paper to land on the doorstep."

"Oh, God," Carla said. "That scared me for a minute."

"Be happy," Stone said, "you just got a big plug from a program the Washington establishment watches every morning, and it didn't blow your story."

"You're right," she said. "I think I'm almost as nervous as Bruce."

Stone took the tray back to the dumbwaiter, and by the time he had rejoined Carla, she was naked again.

"I've got half an hour before I have to get dressed," she said, reaching for him.

"Then let's make the most of it," Stone said, joining her.

# 35

Stone arrived at his desk pretty much on time, and Joan came in. "We've got a little problem," she said, "and you need to make a call."

"What problem?"

"I called Frank Campbell's Funeral Parlor for Bruce about picking up Evan Hills's body and sending it to Philadelphia, but they need a death certificate and permission of a relative."

Stone called Dino.

"Hey."

"Hey, there. I need your help."

"Officially?"

"This time, yes. Will you call the ME and have him issue a death certificate for Evan Hills and release that and the body to Frank Campbell's?"

"At whose request?"

"Mine. I'm Hills's executor."

"That'll do. I'll call him right now." Dino

hung up.

Stone buzzed Joan.

"Taken care of?"

"Yes, you can tell Campbell's to go ahead.
Where is the body being sent?"

"To a Philadelphia funeral director suggested by Campbell's. Bruce didn't know
what else to do."

"Okay."

A few minutes later, Bruce knocked on
the door and came in. "Good morning,
Stone."

"Good morning, Bruce."

"Thank you for helping with the funeral
home. I've called Evan's father's number
twice but haven't been able to reach him."

"Does he know who you are?"

"Very unlikely."

"May I have the father's number?"

Bruce handed it to him. "His name is
Elton Hills." Stone dialed the number but
got only a beep.

"Mr. Hills," he said, "my name is Stone
Barrington. I'm an attorney in New York,
and I'm the executor of your son Evan's
estate. I would be grateful if you would
contact me regarding funeral arrangements." Stone left his number and hung up.
"I hope you slept well."

"Thanks, I did."

Joan buzzed. "I have Mr. Elton Hills on one."

"That was fast." Stone pressed the button. "This is Stone Barrington."

"This is Elton Hills, and I got your message. Are you telling me my son is dead?"

"Mr. Hills, I regret to have to tell you that he is. I'm sorry if my message shocked you. I had thought you would have already heard."

"I don't keep up with the news much. How did he die?"

"In what appears to have been a traffic accident in New York. He was struck by a car while crossing the street."

"When?"

"The day before yesterday. A friend of Evan's arranged for a New York funeral parlor, Frank Campbell's, to transport the body to Philadelphia, to . . ." Joan was standing in the doorway, and she handed him a slip of paper. He read the name of the funeral home to Elton Hills.

"That's fine, they're reliable people. I'll take it from there. You said in your message that you are Evan's executor?"

"That's correct. I'll be glad to send you his letter appointing me and a copy of his will. He hand-delivered it to my office a few hours before his death."

Hills gave him a fax number, and Stone handed it to Joan.

"You should have the fax in five minutes," Stone said. "Please call me if you have any questions."

"Does Evan owe you any money?"

"He gave me a retainer along with his will. That should cover everything. Please let me know if I can be of further help."

"I don't think that will be necessary," Hills said. "Thank you." He hung up.

"How did he sound?" Bruce asked.

"Matter-of-fact. Not upset."

"Evan said he was a pretty cold customer."

"Are you going to Philadelphia?" Stone asked.

"I want to, but not if I'm unwelcome."

Joan buzzed. "Mr. Elton Hills again."

Stone picked up the phone. "Yes, Mr. Hills?"

"Who the hell is Bruce Willard?"

"He's a retired army officer who lives in Washington. He was your son's closest friend. He's in my office now, and he'd like to come to Philadelphia for the funeral."

"Why would he want to do that?"

"As I said, he was your son's closest friend. Would you like his phone number?"

"Yes."

Stone covered the phone. "Your number."

196

Bruce gave him his cell number, and Stone gave it to Elton Hills. "May he expect to hear from you?"

"Let me speak to him."

Stone handed the phone to Bruce. "He wants to talk."

"Hello, Mr. Hills. This is Bruce Willard." He listened, then made writing motions to Stone, who pushed over a pad and pen. "Yes, sir, I've got that. I'll come on Sunday morning. Noon should be fine. Thank you, sir, and please accept my condolences. Evan was a fine man." He handed the phone back to Stone. "He hung up."

"He invited you?"

"To lunch on Sunday. He said the service would be at graveside and private, just him and me."

"Perhaps you'd better take a copy of the Sunday *Times* with you. He said he didn't hear much news. I'll send him a fax, warning him that it's coming."

# 36

Carla got back to Stone's house in the early evening, as he was watching the news. She flopped down on the sofa and requested a martini.

Stone poured the drink. "Is all well?" he asked.

"We closed. All is well."

"Did you find out who called your publisher?"

"Harley David. The meeting was at his house, remember?"

"I remember."

"I added the phone call at the end of the story. It made a good coda." She opened her large bag and withdrew an envelope. "Here's a proof of the piece. Guard it with your life."

Stone opened the envelope, took out some newsprint, and spread it on his desk. "Wow!" he said. "This is impressive."

"It got more column inches than any

investigative piece I've ever worked on. There'll be a lead editorial on the subject, too, but I haven't seen that yet." She took a smaller envelope from her bag and handed it to him. "This is Evan Hills's obit."

"Do you mind if I send all this to his father? He won't receive it until Saturday morning."

"Do you know his father?"

"No, but I spoke to him on the phone this morning. He didn't know his son was dead."

"The old man has a reputation for being reclusive. How did he take the news?"

"Hard to say. Calmly, not to say coldly. He invited Bruce down to lunch on Sunday. The two of them will bury Evan that afternoon."

"No funeral for a sitting congressman?"

"Apparently not. Once Washington has seen your piece, I doubt if there'll be a memorial service at the National Cathedral, either."

"Not unless the Democrats arrange it."

"I suppose that, once your story breaks, there'll be a lot of questions about how Hills died."

"And a lot of inferences drawn, too, I imagine. Have you heard anything from the police about that?"

"No, I haven't talked to Dino today. The

news last night said they had found the offending SUV in New Jersey and that it had been wiped clean of fingerprints."

"I saw that on the AP website," she said. "It was owned by a D.C. security firm."

"Integral Security. Do you know anything about them?"

"Not a thing."

"Have you ever heard of a man called Creed Harker?"

"A lobbyist, I think," Carla said. "I've seen him in the Capitol building. Creepy-looking guy."

"Bruce said he saw Harker in the Four Seasons dining room when you two were having lunch."

"He didn't mention it."

"Bruce thought he was followed to and from your lunch. That's why he's here. He got scared, rented a car, and ran."

"Is he still here?"

"No, he got the shuttle back to D.C. this afternoon, said he had to pack a suit for the funeral on Sunday."

"I liked him. I hope nobody hurts him."

"Oh, damn it, I forgot to give him back his gun."

"Gun?"

"He arrived here packing. I put it in my safe. I'll send it to him."

200

"You can send guns?"

"Sure, just as you can send anything else."

"I hope he doesn't need it."

"So do I."

The phone rang, and Stone picked it up. "Hello?"

"It's Dino. Dinner?"

"Are you batching it again?"

"About every other night."

"Mind if I bring a friend?"

"As long as she's beautiful."

"Never fear."

"The Writing Room at eight? I'll book."

"Right." Stone hung up. "That was my friend the cop. He's invited us to dinner."

"I'm game, but I want a shower and a change of clothes."

"Go do that. I'll watch the news."

They arrived on time at the Writing Room, and Dino was already there. Stone introduced Carla. "Does she qualify?"

"Sure, she does," Dino said, holding her chair.

"Stone, you didn't tell me your cop friend was the police commissioner."

"We go way back," Stone said.

"We were partners about two hundred years ago," Dino said. "I taught him everything."

"Hah!" Stone ejected.

"Anything new on the Hills hit-and-run?" Stone asked.

"I expect you heard we found the car."

"Yep. Anything in it?"

"Clean as a hound's tooth — not even a registration, let alone a print. I'm told it smelled of Windex."

"So the driver's conscience is not clear."

"Nope."

"I wonder if the owner's is."

"It's a small security firm, Integral Security, based in McLean, Virginia."

"Across the Potomac from D.C.," Carla said. "Lot of retired intelligence and military types live there."

"Not a big firm," Dino said, "only five cars registered to them, four Range Rovers and a Mercedes S-type."

"Sounds like a fairly elegant outfit," Carla said. "Are you investigating them further?"

"Not yet," Dino said. "Their car may well have been stolen, who knows? If we get anything contradictory about that, we'll take another look. Stone, do you know how Evan Hills traveled from D.C. to New York?"

"He didn't say," Stone replied. "I assume the shuttle or the train. His friend rented a car and drove up — he thought it was safer," Stone said. "I wonder if Evan did the same."

Dino stepped away from the table and made a call, then came back. "What friend?" he asked.

Stone explained about Bruce Willard. Then they had dinner, and the subject changed. They were on coffee when Dino's phone rang, and he answered. He listened, mostly, then hung up.

"Evan Hills drove his own car, a Cadillac CSX, to New York. His hotel said it was parked at a garage a couple of blocks away. A team is on the way over there now with a flatbed. We'll take it in and have a look at it."

Carla's cell rang, and she listened. "Any idea how they got it?" She hung up. "Four of the congressmen at the meeting have issued statements denying they were there: the Speaker, Thomas Rhea; Robin Ringler, Texas; Nikki Seybold, Ohio; and Gail Barley, Arizona."

"How could they have found out about the story?" Stone asked.

"Who knows?"

"It's a shame we don't have photographs," Stone said.

# 37

The following morning Stone called Elton Hills and left a message: "Mr. Hills, it's Stone Barrington. I'm faxing you two stories that will run in Sunday's *New York Times*. One of them is Evan's obituary, the other is a very important story about a meeting he attended. I thought you should know about it in advance, since it may result in your getting some calls from the media for comment." He asked Joan to cut the big spread into manageable pieces and fax everything.

Dino called. "We pulled in Evan Hills's Cadillac last night and found that the car had been broken into at the garage."

"Was anything stolen?"

"No idea. The registration, an insurance card, and the owner's manuals are all that's there. No prints, either. Smelled of Windex."

"So are you going to treat his death as a

homicide?"

"We've never treated it any other way."

"Have you still got his iPhone?"

"Yeah, I guess."

"Check for photographs on it, will you?"

"Okay."

"When you're done with it, you can release it to me. The car, too."

"Okay. I liked your journalist friend."

"I thought you would."

"But she's based in Washington, right?"

"Right."

"So now you've got two girlfriends in D.C. and none up here."

"That's a depressing way to put it. Carla gets up here fairly often, it seems."

"Speaking of girlfriends, what do you hear from Dolce?"

"Not a thing, and I hope that continues."

"I had a call from Mary Ann this morning . . ."

"No kidding? That's a first, isn't it?"

"I guess so. She had some information about Eduardo's art collection."

Joan buzzed Stone, and he put Dino on hold. "Mary Ann Bianchi on two for you."

"Tell Dino I'll call him back." He pressed the second button. "Good morning, Mary Ann."

"Good morning, Stone," she said. "I had

a very interesting phone call from Dolce this morning. I had told her about the forgeries, and she had a look at the paintings."

"Did she confirm that they are forged?"

"Just the opposite. She said that when she was a girl, studying painting, she copied eight of them as an exercise, and she took large-format, Kodachrome photographs of them to work from. She compared the color transparencies to the paintings, and she says that they are all genuine."

"That's very interesting. Why do you think the appraisers thought they were forgeries?"

"I talked to the chief appraiser: their opinion was based entirely on the little check marks pressed into the frames. In the absence of the check marks, they would have authenticated all the paintings."

"And that's because Charles Magnussen told Raoul Pitt that the check marks meant he had forged them?"

"Yes."

"And that was their only basis?"

"Yes."

"I'll look further into this," Stone said. He hung up and got into his coat; he told Joan to tell Dino he would call him later.

"How long will you be out?" she asked.

"I don't know. I'll call you if it's more than

a couple of hours."

Stone took a cab up to West Fifty-seventh Street and the Pitt Gallery, and asked at the front desk for Raoul. He was soon seated in the gallery owner's office.

"You know, Stone, don't you, that the audit of my gallery and storerooms has been completed and that none of the pictures bear the check marks?" Pitt asked.

"Yes, I know," Stone said. "I've come about something else."

"How can I help?"

"Tell me, in as much detail as possible, about the meeting where Magnussen told you about the check marks."

"His girlfriend, Greta Olafson, called me and told me Charles was dying, so I went to see him at New York Hospital. He was in a private room and obviously in pain."

"Had he been sedated?"

"He said his pain was being managed, but he seemed perfectly lucid to me."

"How did the subject of the check marks come up?"

"I raised the subject of his legacy. I told him that he would be remembered as more than a forger, that he was a brilliant painter. He laughed."

"Why did he think that was funny?"

"I think he disagreed, and he appreciated

the irony that he would be remembered more for his forgeries than his original work. Then he said he had done many forgeries in recent years, and he told me how he had marked them. He said, 'Believe me when I tell you, it's the forgeries that will make me immortal.' "

"Did you believe him?"

"I didn't know whether to or not. He was getting tired, so I said my final goodbyes and left."

"Do you know where his girlfriend is?"

"I believe she's living downtown at Charles's place. He bought a disused commercial building in SoHo twenty years ago. He lived and worked there."

"Let's go and see her," Stone said.

"I'll call her and see if she's available."

"Don't call — let's surprise her."

"All right."

They got a cab downtown and found the building. Raoul rang the bell, and a woman answered the unicom and buzzed them in. They went to the top floor in a freight elevator and stepped off that into a large living room, comfortably furnished. The walls were adorned with what Stone assumed were Magnussen's original paintings, since he didn't recognize any paintings by others.

They were greeted by a striking woman in

her fifties with long, perfectly straight gray hair, and dressed entirely in black. Raoul introduced Stone to Greta Olafson. She seated them and asked a maid to bring them coffee.

"It's a nice surprise to see you, Raoul," she said. "Thank you for coming to Charles's memorial service."

"I'm glad I was there," Raoul replied. "It was nice to hear Charles spoken well of."

"He was a better man than most people knew," she said. "He helped many struggling artists — gave them studio space in the building and, often, stipends."

"That was good of him and perfectly in character for the man I knew."

Coffee came, and the maid served them.

"Why have you come to see me?" Greta asked.

"There's something I want to ask you about," Raoul said. "The last time I saw Charles — when he was in the hospital — we had a brief conversation that puzzled me."

"About what?"

"He said that he had pressed into the wood of some pictures he had restored a little check mark. He said . . ."

Greta began to laugh.

Stone and Raoul exchanged a glance and

waited for her to stop, but she continued to laugh.

Finally, she got control of herself. "That," she said, dabbing at her eyes with a tissue, "was Charles's little joke on the art world."

"Joke?"

"When he restored a picture, he had this little dye, and he tapped on it, leaving the mark on the frame. It amused him to tell me about it."

"Why did it amuse him?"

"I told you, it was his little joke. He didn't tell me why it was funny."

"I think I'm beginning to see," Raoul said.

"Then please explain it to me," she said.

"I think Charles wanted to make some waves in the art world after his death," Raoul said. "He told me he placed the check marks on forgeries he had made when he accepted pictures for restoration."

"Oh, that's ridiculous," Greta said. "After Charles got out of prison, he never did another forgery. I watched him work all the time. I would be working on a sculpture while he was cleaning and restoring the pictures that came to him. He never once copied one of them."

"Well, his little joke worked, at least once. Stone, here, is the executor of Eduardo Bianchi's estate, and the appraisers found twenty-four paintings with the check marks and, having heard the story, thought they were forgeries. It appears they are not."

She began to laugh again. "I can hear him laughing with me," she said. "He would have loved to see their faces when they examined the paintings. They must have thought Charles was an even better forger than he had once been!"

In the cab on the way back uptown, Raoul said, "I think I'll have a word with an art critic at the *Times* I'm friendly with. I believe he will find Charles's little joke to be newsworthy, if not amusing."

"I don't think the appraisers will find it amusing," Stone said, "but I will take great pleasure in telling them about the joke."

# 38

Stone called the head of the art appraisal team and broke the news about the check marks. He was met with silence.

"Hello?" he said finally.

"I'm still here," the woman said. "I don't believe you."

"I've just met with Charles Magnussen's longtime companion, Greta Olafson, and she assures me that, once Charles got out of prison, he never forged another painting. They worked in the same studio, so she would have known. Does that impress you at all?"

"I'm not sure," the woman said.

"Well, you had *better* be impressed, because if you should lend credence to a rumor that the Bianchi collection contains forgeries, I will fall on you and your group from a great height, and no one will ever again purchase your services. Do you understand me?"

"Quite," she said.

"And you may watch the *New York Times* for a thorough debunking of your position and an account of Charles Magnussen's little joke on the art world." He hung up and called Dino. "Call off the art squad," he said.

"I thought I would hear you say that when you broke off our call. You had Mary Ann on the line, didn't you?"

"Yes, and Raoul Pitt and I got the whole story from Magnussen's girlfriend." Stone told him about their trip downtown.

"That's a great story, Stone, you'll dine out on it for years."

"I certainly will."

Stone called Mary Ann, who was greatly relieved to get the news. "I'm delighted, but something else has come up," she said.

"What now?"

"I received a telephone call today from the mother superior of the convent where Dolce recovered from her illness."

"Yes?"

"She told me that Dolce had psychiatric counseling for more than a year after her arrival there."

"I'm glad to hear it. It seems to have worked."

"That's what the mother superior thought,

but apparently it worked a little too well. Dolce and her psychiatrist formed a closer relationship than had been intended. This was confirmed to her by a novitiate who had come upon them *in flagrante delicto* in a storeroom Dolce used as a studio. The psychiatrist was removed from the case at once."

"Why would the mother superior call you about that at this late date?"

"Because she read the name of the psychiatrist in the Italian newspapers," Mary Ann said. "He was a brilliant man in a number of fields, by all accounts, who left Sicily to join the Vatican Bank in an important position. He was an Irish priest named Frank Donovan."

Stone froze in his seat.

"You do read the papers, don't you?" Mary Ann said.

"I'm sorry, yes, I know to whom you are referring."

"Stone, it is very important that Dino not hear about this from you."

"Then from whom should he hear about it? Are you going to tell him?"

"Certainly not, and if you have any respect for the memory of my father and for your duties as his executor, neither will you."

"Mary Ann —"

"Listen to me, Stone. Even if it were known that Dolce knew him, there is nothing whatever to connect them after he went to the Vatican. Nothing."

"Why do you think that?"

"Because if a connection were known, Dolce would already have been questioned by the police."

"I expect that is true, but —"

"No buts," Mary Ann said firmly. "You cannot subject my father's name and his family's reputation to the kind of public scrutiny that would occur if the police could connect Dolce with Father Donovan in any way at all, even if they could be shown never to have met during Father Donovan's brief visit to New York."

"Very brief visit."

"I've spoken to the cardinal, and he assures me that Father Donovan came to New York on Vatican business and stayed at an Opus Dei facility for visiting priests and dignitaries. He made no mention of having seen anyone outside the archdiocese during his stay there. The cardinal believes him to have been a victim of street crime, and that is what I believe, too."

"Then why are you telling me all this?"

"Because I knew that if you or Dino — particularly Dino — heard of the connection between Dolce and Donovan, you would draw the wrong conclusions, and before the investigation was complete, a great deal of harm would have been done to all concerned."

"Except to Father Frank Donovan."

"Especially to the priest, whose reputation would be destroyed, and to the Vatican, which would be greatly embarrassed for no good reason."

"I understand your views, Mary Ann, and I will keep them in mind."

"Please see that you do." She hung up.

Stone hung up, too, shaken and worried.

## 39

Bruce Willard drove his own car, an old Mercedes station wagon that he used mostly for buying trips, to Philadelphia, following the confident instructions of a dash-mounted GPS. He followed the directions numbly, trying not to think of Evan for a while.

As he neared his destination he began looking for a driveway or a mailbox but saw neither. Then the female voice of the GPS began to insist that he make a U-turn. He did so and retraced his track until the U-turn message came again. This time he slowed down to ten miles per hour, but he still nearly missed an overgrown, gravel track: no street number, no mailbox. He turned into the track and proceeded slowly, branches on either side scraping against the car. After a quarter of a mile or so the little road widened and became paved with granite cobblestones, winding through a corridor of old oak trees until he passed through a high, wrought-iron gate and into a forecourt before a large brick house of the Federal style — three stories, the corners and windows trimmed in limestone. The place practically gleamed with good care and fresh paint.

As he came to a halt the front door opened and an Asian man in a white jacket, black trousers, and black bow tie trotted down the front walk to the car.

"Good morning. Mr. Willard?"

"I am," Bruce replied.

"May I take your luggage?"

"There's just the duffel in the backseat."

"I am Manolo," the man said. "I take care of Mr. Hills. Please follow me."

Bruce trailed him up the walk and into the house and a broad foyer containing a Georgian table so beautiful that he had to resist stroking it, upon which rested a heavy silver bowl filled with fresh flowers.

"The living room is to the left," Manolo said, pointing, "and the library to the right. Your room is upstairs." He trotted up the broad staircase and opened the first door down the hallway to the right. "This is the Elm Room," Manolo said. "Mr. Hills hopes you will be comfortable here."

Bruce surveyed the room — the canopied

bed, the comfortable chairs before an Adam fireplace, the good pictures, the fine fabrics. "I'm sure I will be," he said.

Manolo opened the door to a dressing room. "Would you like me to unpack for you?"

"Thank you, that won't be necessary."

"Mr. Hills expects you for lunch in half an hour," the man said. "He will meet you in the library."

"How are we dressing?" Bruce asked. He was wearing a blue suit and a necktie, since he did not know if he would have time or a place to change before the funeral.

"You are perfectly dressed, sir. Is there anything else I may do for you?"

"Thank you, no, Manolo. I'll be down in thirty minutes."

Manolo left, closing the heavy mahogany door softly behind him. Bruce took his toiletry items into the big marble bathroom, splashed some water on his face, then took off his jacket and sat in a comfortable chair for a few minutes, still numb.

At the appointed hour Bruce put his jacket on again, adjusted his necktie, and walked downstairs to the library. A man was sitting at a desk, wielding a magnifying glass, examining an album of stamps. He looked up and stood. "Good afternoon, Mr.

Willard," he said.

Bruce thought he looked exactly as Evan would have looked in thirty years: slim, beautifully tailored, with thick white hair.

Elton Hills came around the desk and offered his hand, then directed Bruce to a wing chair before the large fireplace, where a fire burned brightly. "Would you like a glass of sherry before lunch?" he asked.

"Thank you, yes." He sat down, and a moment later Manolo appeared with a silver tray bearing a black bottle and two glasses. He poured the wine and handed it to Bruce and Mr. Hills, then left.

"It's a fino, nicely chilled," Hills said. "It won't get you drunk before lunch."

Bruce tasted it. "Excellent," he said.

"Have you ever visited Spain?" Hills asked.

"Yes, in fact I once attended the sherry harvest festival in Jerez de la Frontera, as the guest of one of the houses there."

"And did you enjoy the experience?"

"It was a week of relentless debauchery," Bruce replied. "Every time I turned around there was someone with a bottle of sherry, refilling my glass. There was a bullfight, a *fiera,* and in the wee hours, after dinner, much flamenco dancing, much of it by members of my host firm and their domestic staff."

Hills smiled. "I did that once, too — once was enough."

"I know how you feel."

"Tell me, Mr. Willard, was my son a queer?"

"Yes," Bruce replied, "as am I, though these days we prefer 'gay.' We were lovers as well as friends."

Hills winced noticeably. "I was afraid of that."

"Mr. Hills, if you are uncomfortable in my company, I can leave now."

Hills made a placating motion with his hands. "No, please. I'm sorry if I offended you. I'm an old man, unaccustomed to today's ways, and there are many things I don't understand."

"Are you of a religious nature, Mr. Hills?"

"I am."

"Well then, all I can say to you on the subject is that God made us all, and he made us as we are. Evan and I no more chose our sexual orientation than you chose yours."

"You're quite right, I suppose. I didn't choose to be heterosexual, I just was."

"And there you have it in a nutshell."

Manolo entered the room and called them

to lunch. They did not speak again about
sexuality.

# 40

They dined on butternut squash soup and perfectly cooked lamb chops and shared half a bottle of a French wine. The plates were taken away, and while they awaited dessert, Elton Hills began to speak quietly.

"I suppose I could be considered by some as a recluse," he said. "My wife died nearly twenty years ago, and, without really thinking about it, I began to leave this house less and less."

"It's a beautiful house, beautifully kept," Bruce replied.

"Thank you. It was built by my great-great-grandfather, after the American Revolution, and my grandfather and father made judicious additions. I have contented myself with preservation." He took a sip of his wine. "It is my great regret that I secluded myself not only from the outside world, but from my only remaining son. My firstborn, Elton Junior, in a burst of patriotism of which I heartily approved, joined the army and became a platoon leader in Special Forces. He gave his life for his country."

"I'm very sorry for your loss," Bruce said.

"How did you come to be in the military?"

"I was born in a small town in Georgia called Delano," Bruce replied. "As I approached college age, my only alternative was a branch of the state university, but my father had gone to high school with our congressman, and he secured an appointment to West Point for me. I did well there and made my career in the army. I was executive officer of a Special Forces unit when, leading a patrol, I stepped on a land mine. After a year at Walter Reed, I retired. I had saved most of my pay, and I used that to open my shop in Washington."

"I like an entrepreneur," Hills said.

"I'm very impressed with the quality of your pieces in this house," Bruce said. "I would like to specialize in American furniture, but the prices have risen so much that I haven't had the capital to invest. As you know, Evan was very kind to me in his will, and I've thought of funding a furniture operation with some of that."

"What a good idea," Hills said. "You know, once Evan was out of law school, he wouldn't take anything from me. His mother left him a modest bequest, and I was very glad to see that he had grown his estate so much during his life. Now I have no heirs, only a foundation."

Bruce didn't know what to say about that, so he only nodded.

Dessert was served, and Elton Hills changed the subject. "This Mr. Barrington sent me copies of a story about Evan that appears in today's *New York Times,*" he said. "Did you know about all that?"

"Yes, I did. Evan used my shop for meetings with the reporter from the *Times.* I got a copy of the paper last night and read the piece."

"I've been a Republican all my life, and I was absolutely appalled at what I read. My party has returned to being what it was when Teddy Roosevelt was president, and it makes me very sad."

"Evan was outraged," Bruce said, "and frightened of what the reaction would be if those in his party found out where the story originated."

"Do you think Evan's death was . . . not an accident?" Hills asked.

"I think it's possible. Certainly Evan felt endangered. Stone Barrington had offered him a guest apartment in his home, and Evan had accepted. He was on his way to his hotel to collect his things when he was struck by the car."

"If it turns out that Evan was murdered for political reasons, I shall reconsider what to do with the residue of my estate. I think I would use it to help oust from office those who were responsible."

"I can understand your feelings."

Hills consulted a gold pocket watch. "Well, let's not keep the bishop waiting," he said. "We'll take my car, and of course, I would be pleased if you would stay the night."

"Thank you. I'd be happy to."

Hills's car was a Rolls-Royce from the sixties, apparently little used, as it was in showroom condition. The cemetery was only a few minutes' drive from the house, and as they approached the entrance they saw a large van with an antenna on top parked at the front gate. A reporter with a microphone was saying something into a camera, and there were other reporters and photographers there, too.

"Don't slow down," Hills said to Manolo. "Just plow through." As they passed through the gates, the reporters nearly threw themselves in front of the car, and they shouted questions as it passed. Hills sat back in his seat. "Mr. Barrington warned me this might happen," he said, "but I didn't believe him. You've met this Barrington. What do you make of him?"

"I was impressed with him, and so was Evan, enough so to make him his executor. He chose Barrington to tell his story to because he's known to be a friend of the president and his wife, the president-elect. I think he chose well."

The car pulled up behind a police car that was apparently guarding the grave site. A robed bishop stood, waiting for them. Hills greeted the man and had a brief conversation with him, then introduced Bruce. The funeral director appeared and led them to the graveside.

A mahogany casket rested on an apparatus over the grave, covered by a blanket of yellow roses that Bruce had sent.

The service was brief; the bishop spoke for less than five minutes, and Hills indicated that he had nothing to say. Neither did Bruce. It was all over very quickly.

The media still swarmed around the gate, but they got no joy from the people in the Rolls. Soon they pulled into the hidden driveway.

"Bruce, if I may call you that . . ."

"Certainly."

"And please call me Elton."

"Of course."

"Bruce, I wonder if, while you're here, you would take a walk around the house and look at my furniture and art. It has not been appraised for many years."

"I'd be delighted. And if you can endure my company for a few days, I'd be very pleased to do a proper inventory and photograph each piece. A proper appraisal will require some research, but I'm sure your insurers would like to have that, as well as your attorneys."

"What a good idea!" Hills said, smiling for the first time that day. "Come inside, and I'll show you around."

"All I need is a legal pad," Bruce said. "My telephone contains a good camera."

"A phone with a camera? Extraordinary!"

"It's an extraordinary world these days, Elton," Bruce said. "You should see a bit more of it."

The two men went into the house together, arm in arm.

# 41

Stone and Dino had dinner at the Writing Room, and halfway through their drinks, Stone finally brought himself to speak about what was on his mind.

"I've got some news you should know," he said. "I've been asked not to tell you, but I have to."

"Shoot," Dino said.

"When Dolce was first sent to the nunnery in Sicily, she was treated by a priest who was also a psychiatrist, and they began to have an affair, which the mother superior put an end to. The priest's name was Frank Donovan."

"I'm not as surprised as you may think," Dino said. "Donovan's body parts were found in an area no more than a mile out in Jamaica Bay, pretty much in line with a tidal creek that runs up to the Bianchi property, where there's a dock and a boat that Eduardo used to take rides in."

"I don't see how Dolce could have done this alone," Stone said.

"Neither do I. I think I detect the fine Sicilian hand of Pietro in this. There have been rumors about him for decades, and he is devoted to the family. All Dolce would have had to do was ask."

"Is there anything substantial to tie her to Donovan's death?"

"Donovan arrived at JFK Airport three days before he reported in at the archdiocese, and there's no way we can find out whether he stayed at the Opus Dei guesthouse without a search warrant, and the DA is not going to ask a judge for that, based solely on what we suspect."

"You suspect that Donovan was staying with Dolce?"

"The staff in her building clammed up, but one of the younger doormen is on a suspended sentence for assault in a barroom fight, and we were able to lean on him. He ID'd Donovan, said he saw him on the street outside her building, but he wasn't dressed as a priest, and the guy couldn't connect him to Dolce."

"Any security camera shots?"

"Only in the elevator, and a man in a hat would be unidentifiable, because the camera was set high. It's winter, men are wearing hats."

"Have you questioned Pietro?"

"He would go all *omertà* on us, so there's no point. If we pulled him in, that would alert Dolce that we're on to her. I'd rather let her think she's safe."

"Good call," Stone said.

"So we have to wait until she gets mad at somebody else."

"Don't point that thing at me!" Stone said. "You're not using me as bait."

"Why, that never crossed my mind," Dino said, smiling. "But since you bring it up, it's not a bad idea."

"It's the worst idea I've ever heard," Stone said. "You know, I have that house in Paris, now, and I'll move into it if I have to."

"Come on, Stone, wouldn't you like to screw her just one more time? With her head on a pillow, I'll bet she'd spill everything."

"When my time comes, I want to die in bed, but not *her* bed."

"She's living out there alone, now, working in an old stone barn on the property, not far from the creek."

"The farther from me, the better."

"Don't you have any more work to do on the estate?"

"The will has been probated. It's out of

my hands, thank God. How about this? Dolce did some renovation work on that barn. You find out who did the job and interview all the workmen. Maybe somebody saw something."

"That's not the worst idea you ever had," Dino said. "In fact, Mary Ann and I were out there for lunch a decade ago, and there was a painting crew working on the house. If I think about it long enough, I'll remember the name on the truck. Eduardo was the kind of man who'd stick with the same people if he liked their work."

"Now you're talking," Stone said.

"Scali."

"What?"

"Scali — that was the name on the painters' truck."

When Stone got back to his office Joan came in to see him. "The police have finished with Evan Hills's car," she said. "What do you want to do with it?"

"Get me Bruce Willard on the phone, will you?"

She buzzed him a moment later. "Line one."

"Hello, Bruce?"

"Hello, Stone. How are you?"

"Very well. How did the funeral go?"

"It was all very quick — just Elton Hills, me, the undertaker, and the bishop."

"What's Hills like?"

"Actually, we're getting on very well. He asked me to stay for a few days and catalog his furniture, and the job has expanded to the silver and the art, as well. I'm photographing everything and using my laptop to research sale prices on comparable pieces. I should be here for at least a week. Since I only packed for overnight, his housekeeper is doing my laundry every day."

"Did Hills have anything to say about the *Times* piece?"

"He was outraged, just as Evan was. It's very secluded here, there's only one TV, and it's got to be twenty years old and receives through rabbit ears. What's the reaction been in the outside world?"

"A general uproar. The attendees at the meeting are running for the hills. Four of them denied being present at the meeting before the piece even came out. The *Times* has hired Strategic Services, a security company on whose board I serve, to compare the voices on the tape to news tape and interviews, and they might just make some of the attendees that way. Anyway, we have Evan's list of who was there, and all four of the deniers are on the list."

"What has Katharine Lee had to say about it?"

"She and her husband are declining to comment, since there were no laws broken. They're letting the media carry the ball."

"I hope they make lots of touchdowns," Bruce said.

"Bruce, I called about Evan's car. The police have released it. Would you like it sent to you in Washington? I can have it flat-bedded down there. A window needs replacing."

"Yes, please, send it to my garage." Bruce gave him the address.

"A lawyer in my firm's Washington office is handling the will. He says everything is in order, but it may still take a little while. I gave him your number. He'll be in touch."

"Thank you. Listen, I'd better get back to work, there's a lot to do."

"Take care, then."

Joan came back in. "Is Bruce coming to see us again?"

"I don't think so," Stone said.

Joan sighed and went back to her office.

# 42

Dino called in Detective First Grade Carmine Corretti for a chat late in the day.

"How you been, Carmine?" he asked, when he had settled Corretti into a chair and poured him a scotch.

"Pretty good, Commish," the detective said.

"How much longer to retirement?"

"Four months. We bought a condo in Boca."

"Sounds good. Think you've got one more good case in you?"

"I just might be able to muster the strength."

"You spend much time in the neighborhood these days?"

"I still live there."

"You know the old painter guy Scali?"

"Sure. Haven't seen him for a few years. My old man used to play boccie with him. 'Course, the old man is gone now, but he and Stefano Scali were tight."

"You know about the dead Irish priest?"

"The one that turned up in Jamaica Bay in pieces?"

"That's the one."

"I heard about it. Any leads?"

"No leads, but a hunch, maybe."

"You still get hunches, Commish?"

"Yeah, and I still got a few of my own teeth."

"What's your hunch?"

"I think the priest may have been killed in a building up a creek from Jamaica Bay." Dino got a map of the area from his desk and spread it on the coffee table. "The building's right here," he said, pointing at a dot near the creek.

Corretti gazed at the map, then there was a tiny flinch. "I know this location," he said.

"Do you, Carmine?"

"Sure, that's the Bianchi place." He pointed. "The big house is right about here."

"Right. Eduardo died, you know."

"Everybody knows. Who lives in this building you're talking about?"

"Nobody. It's used as an art studio, and it had some recent renovations."

"And Scali painted it?"

"You're way ahead of me, Carmine."

"You think the priest was chopped up there?"

"No, Pietro would have been more careful than that."

"Pietro? That's one sinister guy, you know?"

"I know."

"Why would Pietro want the priest dead?"

"Pietro didn't even know about the priest until he was already dead. I think he might have died in that old stone barn, and if he did, he could have done some bleeding before the body got moved."

"So, you want me to get a warrant and have a look around?"

"No warrant. I just want you to talk to Stefano Scali and see if he noticed anything out of order in the barn. Then get back to me, and we'll see where we go from there."

"Sure, Commish."

"And don't take your partner."

"This gonna be just between us, Commish?"

"Just between us."

Carmine Corretti got home around six and kissed his wife, Gina. "Hey," he said.

"Hey," she replied. "You up for a scotch?" They had one together every evening.

"Yeah, but first I gotta run an errand."

"What kind of errand?"

"I gotta talk to a guy a couple of blocks over, on Mulberry."

"What guy?"

"It's about a case. I can't talk about it."

Gina kissed him on the neck. "You can always talk to me."

"Not this time, babe. I'm doing this for the commissioner, and he wants no talk."

"Secret stuff, huh?"

"Just confidential stuff — you know how it is. I'll be home in half an hour, forty-five minutes."

"I'll keep the ice cubes warm."

Carmine left his house and walked over to where Stefano Scali had his business. The garage door in front was open and Scali and two of his men were sweeping and mopping the floors.

"Carmine!" Scali said, dropping his broom and pumping the detective's hand. "Long, long time. How you doin'?"

"I'm doin' good, Stef. You?"

"Never better."

"Business good?"

"Can't complain. People always need a coat of paint on things. You want a Strega?"

"Thanks, but Gina's expecting me home. I just wanted to ask you something."

"Sure, anything."

"Did you do some work out at Eduardo

Bianchi's place recently?"

"Me and my old man before me been doing Eduardo's painting for forty years."

"Recently?"

"Yeah, the girl turned the old stone barn into an art studio."

"And you painted it?"

"Sure, I did. She's a looker, that girl — *bella, bella*!"

"While you were there, you notice anything out of order?"

"You mean like the toilet, or something?"

"Nah, I mean, like was there a mess or anything?"

"The place was neat as a pin while I was working, and we didn't spill a drop."

"Anybody else spill anything?"

"You mean like food?"

"You see any stains on the floors or walls?"

Stefano thought about it. "Our last day there, we got to work at eight, and there was some stains on the floor. I cleaned 'em up."

"How'd you clean them?"

"I wiped them up, then I used some spray I got to get in the crevices. It's a stone floor."

"You got a blank piece of paper?"

Stefano went to his desk and came back with a clean sheet of paper.

Carmine drew a rectangle. "If this is the

barn floor, where were the stains? Draw an X."

Stefano looked at the rectangle. "There was doors here and here. This wall was the last thing we painted, and the stains were about here." He drew an X. "Just off our drop cloths."

"You said you wiped them first. Was it paint?"

"It was red and sticky, but it wasn't paint. I know paint."

"What did you wipe them up with?"

"A clean rag, I think."

"Have you still got the rag?"

"Nah, I threw it away."

"Where?"

"In the trash can. We're cleaning up this morning — we do it once a week, whether it needs it or not — and we put all the trash in the dumpster out back. We share it with the hardware and the undertaker."

"Let's take a look," Carmine said.

Stefano led him out back and raised the lid on the dumpster. "Them three bags we put there," he said, pointing.

"Can we take 'em inside and have a look?"

"Okay." The two men carried the three trash bags into the shop, and Stefano opened them all. "This one," he said, upending the bag and dumping a lot of rags

240

on the floor.

Carmine took a pen from his coat pocket and moved the rags around. "You said it was a clean one?"

"Yeah. Here, let me do it." Stefano went through the rags and came up with a clean one. Except for two stains, now turned brown.

"Can I have this?" Carmine asked.

"It's trash. You want a clean rag?"

"Nah, this one will do." Carmine produced a plastic evidence bag and stuffed the rag inside.

"What's this about, Carmine?" Stefano asked. "Why are you wanting my rag?"

"I want to see what's on it."

"I'm not getting anybody in trouble, am I? I like the girl. I wouldn't want to cause her any problems."

"How do you feel about Pietro?" Carmine asked.

Stefano made a face and a noise. "He's a snake."

"Did somebody ask you to clean up the stains?"

"No, there was nobody there when we got set up. I saw 'em and cleaned 'em up. The girl didn't get in until later."

"Did she ask about the stains?"

"No, I told her I found them and cleaned

'em up. She had a look at the place on the floor, and said it looked fine. Thanked me, like the lady she is."

"Thanks, Stefano," Carmine said. "I'll let you get back to work."

"Don't make it so long next time?"

"Don't worry, I'll be seeing you."

Carmine went home and had his scotch with Gina, then they had the dinner she had made. The rag could wait until tomorrow.

# 43

Stone got a call from Carla Fontana. "How's it going?" he asked. "Have you been made executive editor yet?"

"Not yet, but the word 'Pulitzer' is being whispered in the hallways around here."

"Have you heard from Strategic Services yet about the voice identifications?"

"They've nailed about half of those on the list, including the four who denied it before the story was published. When the techs have finished, we'll be doing a follow-up piece on the voice comparisons."

"Good luck with that."

"Listen, I called because I haven't been able to find Bruce Willard. Have you heard anything from him?"

"Yes, he's in Philadelphia, visiting Evan Hills's father."

"Elton Hills? The recluse?"

"Bruce went there for the funeral, and he apparently hit it off with the old man. He's spending a few days at his house, cataloging the contents, several generations' worth. Have you left him any messages?"

"No, I just called a couple of times and got voice mail."

"Well, either leave him a message or wait until next week when he's back home."

"Okay."

"Is anything wrong?"

"No, I was just concerned, after what happened to Evan."

"He's fine, don't worry. Now that your story is out, it's too late for them to need to keep him quiet."

"Yeah, you said that before, but I was worried anyway. I'm coming to the city this weekend to see my mother — it's been too long. You want to have dinner?"

"Sure. Where does your mother live?"

"In Brooklyn Heights."

"You want to ask her to dinner with us?"

"Actually, I had a different kind of dinner in mind. Anyway, she's always working."

"What does she do?"

"She's a translator, from French and Italian to English and vice versa."

Stone had a thought. "Is she any good at it?"

"She's highly sought after among publishers, but she'll only work on stuff she finds interesting."

"I might have something interesting for her."

"I'll give you her number. Got a pencil?"

"Shoot." Stone wrote down the number. "What's her name?"

"Anna de Carlo Fontana is her working name. Tell her I sent you."

"Was she born in Italy?"

"Sicily. Her parents brought her to America when she was fourteen. In fact, she was the reason they emigrated. She was very bright, and they wanted her to have a good education and more opportunity. What do you need translated?"

"Just some old documents. It's a legal matter, and I can't discuss it."

"Okay, I'll be in Friday morning. I've got some meetings at the *Times* that could take all day."

"Can we make a weekend of it?"

"I like the way you think. Bye-bye." She hung up.

Stone dialed the Brooklyn number.

The phone was answered immediately. "Yes?"

"Mrs. Fontana?"

"Yes."

"My name is Stone Barrington. I'm an attorney in the city."

"How do you do?"

"Very well, thank you. Your daughter, Carla, suggested I call you about doing some translation."

"Very nice of her to send work to her mother. What do you need translated?"

"It's an old journal, written in what I'm told is a Sicilian dialect."

"Whose journal?"

"A friend of mine who passed away recently."

She was quiet for a moment. "Was he very old?"

"He died at ninety-four."

"Eduardo Bianchi?"

"That was a very good guess."

"Not really. I knew him when I was younger. I saw his obituary in the *Times.*"

"Would you like to come to my office and have a look at the journal?"

"Yes, I would. Coming from Eduardo, I expect it must be very interesting."

"I expect it will be. I would be grateful if you would keep this conversation in the strictest confidence."

"If you like. When?"

"As soon as you like."

"This afternoon? I'm delivering a manuscript to a publisher in the city."

246

"That would be fine." He gave her the address.

"Around three o'clock?"

"Very good. I'll look forward to seeing you."

"Same here." She hung up.

# 44

Carmine showed up for his appointment with the commissioner the following afternoon.

"How'd you do?" Dino asked.

"I did perfect."

"How perfect?"

"Stefano said he found some red stains on the floor of the old stone barn, and he cleaned them up on his own, without being asked. The girl was pleased."

"We need more than that."

"He used a clean rag for the cleaning," Carmine said, holding up the evidence bag.

"Great. Now run the DNA against Frank Donovan."

Carmine put an envelope on Dino's desk. "Done. A one hundred percent match."

"Great! Have you done all the paperwork to preserve the chain of evidence?"

"Done." Carmine handed him another envelope.

"You done perfect, Carmine."

"Ain't that what I said?"

"Did you tell Scali he's going to have to testify to this?"

"Not exactly. He's not going to want to testify against Eduardo's daughter, though."

"Then you have to persuade him."

"Thing is, he won't have a problem with testifying against Pietro. We'll get him in front of a grand jury for that, then the DA can throw in the questions about the girl."

"We don't have anything against Pietro, unless he confesses or Dolce testifies, and neither of those things is going to happen."

"We know that, but Scali don't."

"What will the questions be?"

"We'll lead him through his arrival at work that morning and ask him if he found anything amiss. He'll say he found the stains and cleaned them up, then we'll ask him if the girl was aware of that, and he'll say he told her."

"That's not so good. I wish she had seen the stains and asked Scali to clean them up."

"Wishing ain't gonna make it happen, but we can put Donovan in her studio, bleeding. That ought to be good enough for a search warrant, then we can look at stains with luminol and at any knives in the place."

"It only proves that Donovan did some

bleeding there, not that Dolce made him do it. And anyway, we got a problem with getting a warrant, Carmine."

"What problem?"

"The archdiocese. No ADA is going to want to go up against those guys, not unless we've got conclusive evidence."

"In which case we wouldn't need a warrant."

"Right."

"So, if we have the evidence, we don't need a warrant, and if we don't have the evidence, we need a warrant to get it. What's that called?"

"A pain in the ass," Dino said.

"Maybe if you called the cardinal and explained it to him he'd go along. After all, it's one of his people who got murdered."

"More than that, it's one of the *Vatican's* people."

"Well, then?"

"Carmine, if we go into that we're going to have to go into Dolce's relationship with Donovan, and that is not going to sit well with the archdiocese *or* the Vatican."

"I must be missing something here," Carmine said. "What relationship?"

"This goes back a while. Dolce was certifiable, but instead of putting her into a loony bin, Eduardo shipped her to a convent in

250

Sicily, where Donovan was her psychiatrist."

"He was a priest *and* a psychiatrist?"

"Right: two men in one, and neither of them should have been fucking Dolce, but both of them were."

"Sheesh!"

"If you'd ever seen Dolce, you'd understand why. Anyway, the mother superior figured it out and got Donovan pulled from Dolce's case, but we don't know exactly what she said to the higher-ups to make that happen. And can you imagine issuing a subpoena to a mother superior in Sicily to testify before a grand jury?"

"No," Carmine said, shaking his head vigorously. "I cannot imagine that."

"Neither can I."

"So, Commish, you're saying we're fucked?"

"For the moment, yes. We need more, and I don't know how we're going to get it."

"Well," Carmine said, getting to his feet, "let me know if there's anything else I can do."

"I'd assign you to the case officially, if I thought there was some point," Dino said.

"Then I'll leave it in your hands, Commish." Carmine shook the boss's hand and excused himself, but he was not happy about the way this had gone. He was within an ace of going into retirement with the solving of a huge case on his record, maybe even a promotion, which would up his pension, which he could use.

This was not right.

# 45

Stone could see where Carla got her beauty. Her mother, Anna, who must be in her seventies, he reckoned, was a knockout: lots of nearly white hair, beautifully coiffed; nicely made up; manicured; wearing an Armani suit.

"Good afternoon," Anna said, offering her hand.

"Good afternoon, Mrs. Fontana. It's a pleasure to meet you."

"Please, call me Anna — even my daughter does."

"And I'm Stone."

"This is a nice legal nest you have here," she said, looking around. "Are you a one-man practice?"

"No, I'm a partner in the firm of Woodman & Weld, but I prefer working here."

"I don't blame you," she said. "Is that the journal?" she asked, nodding toward the stack of red leather volumes on Stone's coffee table."

"That's it."

"May I see the first volume?" she asked.

Stone went to the table, brought back the volume, and handed it to her.

She leafed through it. "I recognize Eduardo's handwriting," she said. "He wrote me many letters."

"So you won't have any trouble reading it?"

"Nor trouble translating it," she said. "How many volumes are there?"

"Eight. How long do you think it would take you?"

"Let me explain how I work," Anna said. "First, I read through the volume and make notes on particular passages, then I sit at my computer and type the manuscript in English as I read it in Italian."

"What word processing software do you use?"

"WordPerfect. It's not as popular as it used to be, but I've never used anything else."

"Many law firms still use it, and we have it here."

"You understand that I'd want to work at home, as I always do?"

"What do you usually charge for translating a book?" Stone asked.

"For a novel of three hundred and fifty to four hundred pages, twenty-five thousand dollars."

"I'll pay you fifty thousand dollars to translate the journal, but there are conditions."

"What conditions?"

"First, you sign and keep a very strict confidentiality agreement. Second, you work in an office here — there's an empty one next door with a computer. Third, you never remove so much as a page from this office, and you make only one backup copy and leave it here at all times."

"May I see the office?"

Stone rose and took her down the hall to the office once used by an associate from Woodman & Weld. She looked around, sat in the chair, switched on the computer and typed a few sentences.

"Satisfactory?"

"Yes, and I like the chair so much I think I'll get myself one."

"How long do you think it will take you to make the translation?"

"If I work, say, six hours a day, perhaps three weeks."

"That seems quite quick."

"Remember, it's a handwritten journal, not typed, so when it's typed on the computer the number of pages will come down."

"Are you translating anything else at the moment?"

"I just turned in a manuscript. I've been sent a couple of others, but I can turn them down to do this."

"Do you accept my terms?"

"Yes, I believe they are fair. One thing, should the manuscript or any part of it ever be published, I want full credit as translator, my name on the cover, if it's a book."

"Agreed."

"Then I can start tomorrow morning at ten."

"That's fine. I'll have my driver run you back to Brooklyn Heights."

"Thanks, but I'd rather take the subway — it's faster."

Joan came to the door and Stone introduced the two women. "Anna is going to be translating Eduardo's journal," Stone said. "She'll be here every day at ten, until she's done. Please write her a check for twenty-five thousand dollars, and when she's done there'll be another twenty-five thousand due. And print out a confidentiality agreement for Anna to sign."

Joan went back to her office.

"Tell me," Anna said, "are you and my daughter an item?"

"We first met in Paris last month, when she interviewed me. We've seen each other a couple of times when she has been in New York. In fact, she'll be here this weekend."

"What a lucky girl," Anna said, making Stone laugh. "She's probably going to get a Pulitzer, too. If so, it will be her second."

"She deserves it."

Joan came back with the check and the agreement; Anna put the check into her purse and signed the agreement. "See you tomorrow," she said.

"We'll look forward to having you here," Stone replied.

He helped her on with her coat and she left.

Stone went back to his office and locked the volumes of Eduardo's journal in his safe again.

## 46

Bruce Willard got home at midday, having completed his cataloging of Elton Hills's furniture, silver, and art. He left his bag in his apartment, then went down to his shop. His assistant, Pamela West, was at her desk in the little office.

"Everything quiet?"

"A customer in the back. He's been in a couple of times while you were gone."

"What's he looking for?"

"He always says he's just browsing."

"I'll have a word with him." Bruce walked to the rear of the store and found a man closely inspecting a Georgian silver gravy boat. He was tall, slim, and bald; he turned to look at Bruce and showed a face with narrow eyes and no eyebrows.

"Good morning," Bruce said, offering his hand. "I'm Bruce Willard. Can I help you with anything?"

The man shook it. "I'm Creed Harker,"

he said with a small smile. "I'm just browsing, really."

"Do you have a particular interest in Georgian silver?"

"I have a particular interest in beautiful things," Harker said.

"Well, we have a shop full of those. Anything you see interest you?"

"I like the portrait hanging over there by the door," he said. "It looks vaguely like a Sargent."

"That's because it *is* a Sargent," Bruce said. "Or, at least, a number of people with knowledge of his work think it is. Of course, a number of people think it isn't. It's not signed, and it appears to be an early work, before his style was fully formed. That's why it's a bargain."

"How much of a bargain?"

"Six thousand dollars."

"Not that much of a bargain."

"If it's a Sargent, it's a screaming bargain."

"What's its provenance?"

"Unknown. I bought it in a mixed estate sale. There are times when you have to rely on your own eye."

"You're a friend of Evan Hills, aren't you?"

"I was. Perhaps you haven't heard that he died two weeks ago."

"I believe I had heard that."

"He was killed in New York by a coward in a car, who then fled the scene."

Harker flushed slightly. "How tragic," he said.

"More than you know. There's a large-scale police investigation, though, and they've already found the car, a black SUV with a Virginia registration."

"I see."

"It was reported stolen, after the fact. What business are you in, Mr. Harker?"

"Private security."

"Would that be Integral Security of McLean?"

"Oh, you know us?"

"I know that your company owned the SUV in question."

"Yes, it was stolen out of our parking lot."

"That doesn't speak very well for your security, does it?"

Harker's eyes were darting about now, as if he were looking for an escape route.

"What did you think of the story in last Sunday's *Times* about Evan and the meeting he attended?"

"I didn't read it," Harker replied.

"Would you like some details? I believe a number of your acquaintances attended the meeting in question."

"Everyone I know denies being there."

"Evan took very good notes," Bruce said, "and he knew all the attendees personally. He also made a recording."

Harker's eyes widened slightly. "How interesting."

"It's going to get a lot more interesting when all the voices have been identified."

"Well, if you'll excuse me . . ." Harker began to edge toward the door.

"No interest in the putative Sargent?"

"Not at this time," he said.

"I'm going to see you in prison, Harker," Bruce said conversationally.

"What?"

"You were driving the SUV, weren't you?"

"That's preposterous!"

"It's highly likely," Bruce said. "Better odds than the Sargent, even."

"You're mad," Harker said, backing toward the door.

"I'm *very* mad," Bruce said, "and don't you forget it."

Harker got the door open and walked quickly away.

"What was that all about?" Pamela asked.

"If he comes back in here, tell him to get out."

"Why?"

"Because I think he's mixed up in Evan's

death. If I see him again, I might kill him, and although I'd love to do it, I don't think it's a very good idea."

"Oh, you had this message," she said, handing him a slip of paper. "Elton Hills would like you to call him as soon as possible."

Bruce went upstairs and called Elton Hills; the phone was picked up on the first ring. "Bruce?"

"Yes, Elton. You called?"

"I had a rather disturbing phone call after you left this morning."

"From whom?"

"A man called Harker, who said he knew Evan. He said he thought I might need protection, and he runs a security company."

"He was just in my shop," Bruce said. "His company owns the vehicle that ran down Evan in New York, and I have a strong feeling that he may have been involved."

"Good God!"

"Please don't speak with him again, Elton. I think he's up to no good."

"What could he possibly want from me?"

"I don't think we want to find out," Bruce said.

## 47

Carmine Corretti got into his gum boots and a windproof jacket. It was a calm day, but chilly outside, so he had worn a thick, Irish fisherman's sweater.

His wife came in from the grocery store. "What are you doing home so early?" she asked. "And what are you doing in those clothes?"

"I'm going fishing," he replied. "And don't ask."

"Do I have to tell you what time of the year it is?"

"The fish don't know that."

"Carmine, this doesn't make any sense."

"I told you not to ask," he said. "I'll be home late this evening, probably around ten." He slipped a spray can of something into a pocket, grabbed his tackle box and a rod, and headed out the door. She was still calling his name when it slammed.

An hour later, Carmine parked his car,

went down to a dock owned by a friend, got into the friend's Boston Whaler, and headed out into Jamaica Bay. The day was clear and calm, or he wouldn't be doing this, he told himself. The sun was sinking into the Atlantic; there wasn't a lot of daylight left. In the dusk he checked the GPS unit and turned into the creek. Lights were on at the big house, and he could see a dock ahead. As he passed the dock he saw lights through some trees; that would be the old barn. He continued up the creek with the rising tide, which would turn soon, and kept looking back. As he turned the boat around he saw the lights go out in the barn.

He pulled the throttle back to idle, keeping just enough way on to steer toward the floating dock, where Eduardo's mahogany runabout was tied up. He cut the engine, glided to the inside of the dock, and grabbed a cleat. He secured the Whaler and climbed out onto the float, then took the catwalk to the pier to which the float was attached. A flagstone path led into the dark woods. He took a small flashlight from his pocket but didn't turn it on yet; he stuck to the path and let his eyes become accustomed to the darkness. The light from a quarter moon helped a little.

He reached the barn and stepped behind

some shrubs to look through a window. The wan moonlight through the skylights gave shape to some furniture and an easel. The place was deserted. He went back to the front door and played the thin beam of his flashlight on the lock. Nothing impenetrable. He took a small wallet from an inside pocket, unzipped it, and removed a set of lock picks that he had made from a hacksaw blade. It had been a while since he had used the tools, but the lock took only a couple of minutes. He let himself in and closed the door softly behind him.

He padded around the place for a few minutes, checking the kitchen, where he found a wooden block holding a set of sharp knives. She had the means, and he had no doubt about motive and opportunity. He went back to the studio and found, roughly, the spot Stefano Scali had marked on his drawing. It looked clean, but Carmine wasn't finished. He removed a small can from his coat pocket and began spraying the contents evenly on the stone floor, then he stopped and turned off his flashlight. Nothing. He moved along a couple of feet and sprayed again. Still nothing. He backed up and went the other way, and this time he had results: a trail of luminescent blue ran for about fourteen inches.

Carmine took out his iPhone and took some pictures; they were remarkably good, he thought. He put the camera back into his pocket and straightened up. As he did, he felt something poke into his back, and a voice said, "Shhhhh." Then, before he could react, someone grabbed his coat collar and held it, then drove the blade into his back. He jerked his body around, but between the grasp on his collar and the pressure on the blade, he was kebabed, so he couldn't turn. Then he was tripped and forced to the floor.

Carmine felt his only chance was to go limp, to seem less of a threat. He was dragged toward the door, then outside onto the stone walk, where he was stopped. Then the blade was withdrawn and his body began to gush. In a moment, he had passed out.

When Carmine awoke he was in a different place; it was moving, and he felt the vibration of an engine. He tried to move just slightly, but could not. There was plastic sheeting over his face, inhibiting his breathing. He wasn't thinking very clearly, but he knew he didn't have long to live; either the bleeding or Jamaica Bay would end it for him.

The boat continued its passage while Carmine fought to stay conscious. Twice more he fainted and came to again, then he stopped struggling to breathe.

He thought about his wife until he passed out again. He never felt the cold water close over him.

# 48

Elton Hills, at the behest of Bruce Willard, had subscribed to the *New York Times* and the *Washington Post,* and he was enjoying the reading. Then, in the social pages of the *Post,* a name in a caption below a photo of a group at a party caught his eye: Creed Harker.

He counted the names and the faces, and his finger came to one floating a head above the rest of the group. He felt the blood rise in him; his ears burned. With no other evidence than what he had heard about Harker and the man's appearance, he felt he had met his enemy. For the first time in years, except for his son's burial, he began to think of leaving his property.

Bruce Willard was at his desk going over a printout of his accountant's monthly profit/loss statement, when the phone rang, and he picked it up. "Bruce Willard."

"Bruce, it's Elton Hills," a voice said.

"Good morning, Elton. I hope you're well."

"I am, thank you. Bruce, I was thinking I might come to Washington for a few days to see how Evan lived."

"What a good idea. I've got the keys to Evan's house. I think you'd be very comfortable there."

"I was hoping you'd say that. I don't think I could tolerate the crowds at a hotel."

"Evan has a live-in couple who take care of the place very well. I'll let them know you're coming."

"That would be grand. Do you think there'd be room for Manolo, too? I'd want him to drive me."

"Of course. When would you like to arrive?"

"Late this afternoon? Would that be all right?"

"Of course. I'll take you to dinner."

"Do you think you could find a quiet table at the Four Seasons in Georgetown? I've heard about the restaurant from you and seen photographs of it in the papers."

"Certainly. They know me there, as they knew Evan. When you arrive in town, come to my shop. I'd like you to see it. Then I'll take you over to the house — it's not far."
He gave the old man the address, then hung

up and called the house to alert the couple that a guest was coming. "It's Evan's father," he said, "and his chauffeur. I hope you'll make them very comfortable."

"Will you require dinner, Mr. Bruce?" the woman asked.

"No, we'll be going out, but after that you should be prepared to serve meals. Mr. Hills doesn't enjoy going out a lot."

"We'll be ready."

Bruce hung up and went back to reading his statements. An hour later, UPS arrived, bringing him a package from Apple Publishing.

"Mr. Hills," Manolo said, "the people you were expecting from your attorney's office have arrived."

"Please show them in, Manolo."

"Yes, sir."

"And, Manolo, I want you to drive me to Washington, D.C., immediately after lunch. Pack a bag for two nights."

Manolo was momentarily speechless; he had never had such a request from his employer. "Yes, sir," he was finally able to say.

"And perhaps you'd better clean the car and fill it with gas."

"Yes, sir." Manolo showed the group of

people into the library, and they began to hand Elton documents.

"Please read the marked passages, Mr. Hills," the attorney said. "Those are where the changes you wished have been made. If they are correct, you may sign them, and we'll witness them properly."

Hills read the documents, approved them, and signed them. The group lined up to witness them.

Before lunch, Elton Hills did something he had not done for many years: he packed a bag. After lunch, he handed the bag to Manolo, then called him to look at a photograph in a folded newspaper. "Do you see this man, Manolo?"

"Yes, sir, very tall, isn't he?"

"I believe so. I'm going out to dinner tonight with Mr. Willard, to a place this man frequents. If you see him arrive, come inside and tell me."

"Yes, sir."

"Then follow him. I want to know where he goes."

"Yes, sir."

"We'll be staying at my son's house tonight. I'm told we'll be very comfortable there."

"Very good, sir." Manolo took the bag to the car and put it into the trunk.

Elton went to his desk, opened a drawer, and removed an object he had owned for more than fifty years. He put it into his coat pocket, got his overcoat, then went to join Manolo in the car.

Elton got into the rear seat of the old Bentley with his newspaper. He was nervous about the trip, but curious about what he might see. They left the estate, and he was amazed at the amount of traffic on the roads, particularly the interstates. They moved at thrilling speeds — seventy, sometimes, at his urging, eighty miles an hour.

This was fun!

## 49

Dino was having a rare lunch at his desk when his secretary buzzed him. "There's a woman on the phone called Gina Corretti. She says you know her."

"Sure." Dino picked up the phone. "Gina? How you doing?"

"Hey, Dino, not so good. Carmine didn't come home last night."

"Has he ever done that before?"

"Not without calling. I called his precinct, and they haven't heard from him since he signed out yesterday. He came home and got his tackle box and a couple of rods and said he was going fishing."

"At this time of year?"

"Go figure. He was wearing rubber boots and a heavy, waterproof jacket."

"Does Carmine own a boat?"

"No, but he sometimes goes fishing with a friend of his who has one. I called him, and he hasn't heard from Carmine since last summer."

Dino began to get a bad feeling. "Gina, do me a favor. Call the friend back and ask him to check on his boat."

"Sure." Gina hung up.

By the time Gina called back, everything had fallen into place in Dino's mind. "What'd he say?"

"He checked at the marina. A guy who said he's a friend of his took the boat. Sounds like Carmine. The boat is a Boston Whaler, eighteen feet with a forty-horsepower outboard."

"Okay, I'm going to check this out, Gina, but it might be a while before I can get back to you." Dino buzzed his assistant. "Call the Coast Guard and see if anybody has reported a Boston Whaler found in Jamaica Bay or around there." Half an hour later, his assistant buzzed back.

"They found such a boat this morning, aground on one of those little islands in the bay. It had some bullet holes in the bottom, but Whalers are almost impossible to sink. And, boss, there was some blood in it. Could be fish blood, but I called Corretti's precinct, and they're sending some people out there."

"Keep me posted," Dino said. He hung up and called Stone.

"Hey."

"We got a problem," Dino said.

"What problem?"

"Dolce."

"Oh, shit. What's happened?"

"I think one of my detectives went out to the Brooklyn property, and he didn't come back. The Coast Guard found his boat." Dino filled him in on what he knew.

Bruce Willard received Elton Hills at his shop and gave him the tour. A lot of what the shop had to offer was in line with what Elton had in his house, and he seemed to enjoy it. When they were done, Bruce rode over to Evan's town house with Elton. The old man took an even greater interest in what Evan had collected.

"Did you find all these things for him?" Elton asked, stroking a piece of silver.

"Many of them, but Evan's tastes were in place before we met. I think he must have inherited them from you."

"More likely, his mother," Elton said.

Bruce led him to the best guest room. "This is quite handsome," Elton said, looking around. "I can sleep here."

The woman who took care of the place brought them tea in the library. Bruce poured.

Elton accepted a cup, added lemon and sugar, and sat back in his chair. "Did I tell you that I served in the Korean war as a young man?"

"No, you didn't."

"I was a platoon leader in the battle of Chosin Reservoir."

"That was a bad one," Bruce said.

"I was a first lieutenant. When our command post took an artillery shell, I suddenly found myself a regimental commander. We made a fighting retreat, and the best I can say for myself was that I got most of the regiment out."

"That says a very great deal," Bruce said. "We studied that battle at the Point, so I have some idea of what you must have gone through."

"It wrecked me," Elton said. "They sent me home with a decoration, and I spent four months in a military hospital, getting the experience off my chest."

They sipped their tea in silence. Bruce wondered why on earth Elton had brought up his military service.

Dino rang the bell at Mary Ann's apartment, and she opened the door.

"Come in," she said, "and tell me about it. Anybody want a drink?"

"No, thanks," Dino said, and Stone shook his head. They threw their coats over a chair and sat down.

Mary Ann sat in a chair, her hands tightly clasped in front of her. "What has Dolce done? Has she been worrying you, Stone?"

Stone shook his head.

Dino spoke up. "It appears that Dolce has murdered two men: one, a Catholic priest, the other an NYPD detective."

Mary Ann got up, crossed the room to a drinks cart, poured herself a stiff scotch, then she came back, sat down, and waited wordlessly for Dino to continue.

She looked frightened, Stone thought, something he would never have imagined of Mary Ann.

"The priest was also a psychiatrist who treated her when she was in Sicily. The cop was looking into his death on his own time."

"Was the priest the one who was found in the bay?"

"Yes."

"Dear God in heaven! Are you certain of all the facts?"

"No, I'm not," Dino said, "but I know enough to know that she did these things or had Pietro do them."

"Are you going to arrest Dolce?"

"We don't have a case in either instance,"

Dino said. "If we wait until we do, then it's going to be the biggest story in the news for a month."

"We can't have that," Mary Ann said.

"No, we can't," Dino replied. "Here's what we can do."

While Mary Ann finished off the scotch and poured another, Dino outlined what he had in mind.

# 50

Elton Hills repeated his earlier instructions to Manolo, then entered the Four Seasons Hotel in Georgetown on the arm of Bruce Willard, his eyes flitting from face to face as they passed through the lobby and into the restaurant.

Bruce had requested a quiet table, and they got one near the hallway that contained the restrooms.

Elton sat quietly and sipped a bourbon while Bruce ordered for him. Before leaving Evan's house, the old man had removed his .45 caliber general officer's pistol, a battlefield souvenir from his demolished command post in Korea, from his pocket, emptied it, then cleaned every accessible part of it, including the individual cartridges. He then reloaded it, worked the action, and let the hammer down to a half-cock, then he wrapped it in his handkerchief and returned it to his coat pocket.

"Well, Elton," Bruce said, interrupting his reverie, "what do you think of the Four Seasons?"

"It's very modern, isn't it?" Elton replied. "Of course, given my absence from the scene for so long, almost everything looks modern. Georgetown looks much the same as when last I saw it, except that it's cleaner, and the trim on the buildings is more freshly painted. It looks much like the way I keep my house."

"I think that's a good assessment," Bruce said. He handed Elton the book he had prepared of his home's furnishings. "I thought you might like to have this."

Elton removed the brown paper wrapping and leafed through the book. "This is quite lovely," he said. "It makes me look at my home afresh."

"I'm glad you like it."

"Bruce, there's something I have to tell you."

"Please do, Elton."

"I made a new will this morning. I've come to have a fatherly feeling for you, and I would have made you a substantial bequest, had not Evan already done so."

"That's quite all right, Elton. I would have expected nothing."

"I didn't say I left you nothing. I know

that, since I don't have an heir, the substance of my estate will go to my family foundation."

"Yes?"

"However, the sale of my possessions is within my gift, and I have appointed you as my agent to conduct the sale of my furniture, silver, art, library, and personal effects, by whatever means you deem advisable, at a commission of forty percent."

"That's extraordinarily generous of you, Elton."

"Not really. It costs me nothing and my estate only what it would cost for an agent if I didn't know you. I did this because I think you might guide my things into the hands of sympathetic owners."

"I will endeavor to do that, Elton."

"There, I feel better now. There is some satisfaction in having prepared for my death. I'm not the sort to leave loose strings dangling."

"I understand how you feel," Bruce said. "I, myself, try to be prepared for that at all times, though I'm fairly young by today's standards and very healthy."

Manolo suddenly appeared at tableside, apologized for the intrusion, and whispered something into Elton's ear. Elton's eyes widened a bit, but he gave no other outward sign of anything out of the ordinary. Elton thanked him, Manolo left, and Elton said, "Manolo wanted me to know that he found a parking place near the door, so we won't have to hunt for him when we leave."

"That was very thoughtful of him."

"Bruce, will you excuse me for a moment? I'd like to wash my hands before dinner."

"Of course."

Elton went down the hallway toward the men's room; it was quiet until a waiter opened the kitchen door, then it was noisy, until the door closed again. He noticed that the door was covered in tufted leather. He walked into the men's room and saw that the inside of the door and the walls were covered in the same tufted leather; it was dead quiet in the room. Then he heard the sound of toilet paper unrolling and noticed that the door of the last stall was closed. He took the pistol, still wrapped in his handkerchief, from his coat pocket and rapped on the stall door.

"There's a free one next door," a voice responded, sounding irritated.

"I believe you dropped something of value out here," Elton said. "If you'll unlatch the door, I'll hand it to you."

There was a cranky noise from behind the door, then it opened to reveal Creed Harker standing there, holding up his trousers with one hand. "What the hell?" he said.

Elton pushed him, and he fell backward onto the toilet seat. Elton pointed the pistol at him. "Hands on your head," he said.

Harker looked terrified, but he put his hands on his head.

Elton reached out and pinched Harker's nostrils. When he opened his mouth to breathe, Elton cocked the pistol, inserted its barrel into the open mouth, and pulled the trigger.

Harker's brains exploded against the wall behind him, and he slumped to one side. Elton took Harker's hand and wrapped it around the pistol, then let it fall to the floor. Elton backed out of the stall, pulled the door shut, and with a small penknife from his pocket, he lowered the inside latch into place. He washed his hands thoroughly and made sure that none of Creed Harker had stuck to him, then he turned and walked out of the men's room, folding the handkerchief and slipping it into his pocket. He doubted if the noise of the pistol had made it past the tufted walls. A moment later he sat down across from Bruce.

"Dinner will be here in a moment," Bruce said.

"I'm looking forward to it," Elton replied, smiling.

Bruce wondered why he suddenly looked so happy.

They were well into their main course when a man came running from the men's room, looking for someone. He disappeared in the direction of the front desk.

Elton looked at his wristwatch; some twenty minutes had passed since he had left the men's room. He reckoned there had been other visitors who had taken no notice of the last stall.

A couple of minutes later, a pair of uniformed police officers appeared outside the dining room; they were followed by plain-clothes types and, eventually, by men with a stretcher. An out-of-order sign appeared at the entrance to the hallway.

"Looks as though something has happened in the men's room," Bruce said.

"Oh?"

A man wearing a badge on his belt approached their table. "Excuse me, gentlemen, can you tell me if you saw anyone go into the men's room recently?"

"My back is to the men's room," Elton said politely.

Bruce looked at Elton, then at the police officer. "No, I didn't," he replied. The officer moved on to the next table, then he came back. "Excuse me, sir, but someone at another table says that you went into the men's room."

"Well, that isn't what you asked me, is it?" Elton said irritably. "I went in there, perhaps half an hour ago, urinated, washed my hands, and came back to my table."

"Is that so?" the detective asked Bruce.

"It is. Did something happen in the men's room?"

"Someone needed medical attention."

"I saw no one else when I was in there," Elton said. "I hope that's helpful."

The officer thanked them, then left the table, apparently satisfied.

Later, on the way out of the hotel, Elton dropped his soiled handkerchief into a trash bin, then got into the waiting Bentley.

"If you don't mind, Elton, I'll walk," Bruce said. "It's a nice evening, and I like to window-shop on the way home from here, to see what the competition is offering."

"Of course," Elton said. "I'll be going home first thing in the morning, but I'll be in touch."

The two men shook hands, and the Bentley drove away.

As Bruce started to walk away, the police

detective who had spoken to them earlier appeared at his side. "Excuse me," he said. "Can you give me the name of the gentleman who was dining with you?"

"His name is Elton," Bruce replied.

The man wrote down the name in a notebook. "Do you think he might have noticed that something might have been amiss in the men's room?"

"Well, he certainly has his wits about him, but he's in his late eighties, and somewhat reclusive. I doubt if he's been in a public men's room for the past thirty years."

"Thank you," the man said, and went away.

Bruce wondered why he had not asked for his name and why he had given the policeman only Elton's first name.

# 51

Bruce Willard woke at his usual 6:30 AM, brushed his teeth, then went to his little kitchen and made coffee, poured orange juice, and toasted himself a muffin, as he did every day of the week, except weekends, when he made himself scrambled eggs and bacon.

He retrieved the *Washington Post* and the *New York Times* from his front doorstep, then went upstairs and took his tray back to bed. At the stroke of seven AM he switched on the TV to the morning CBS TV show and watched as he ate his muffin and sipped his coffee. He finished with the orange juice just as the network handed off to the local news show. A beautiful young woman gazed into the camera and read from a tele-prompter:

"Last night at the swank Georgetown Four Seasons Hotel, a well-known lobbyist and security expert, Creed Harker, died in the men's room of the hotel's restaurant, apparently at his own hand." They switched to tape of the police officer Bruce had spoken with the evening before. "This is only preliminary," the detective was saying, "but we found Mr. Harker's body locked in a men's room stall. He had received a gunshot wound that appears to have been self-inflicted. We found a loaded semi-automatic pistol on the floor beside his body, and his fingerprints were on the gun. A single shot had been fired."

Bruce gulped his orange juice. This could not be happening.

At police headquarters, Detective Avery Morris was called into his captain's office, along with his partner and their lieutenant.

"Are we ready to wrap this up?" the captain asked.

The lieutenant turned to Morris. "Avery? Bring us up to date."

Morris nodded. "We processed the men's room last night and found nothing to indicate the presence of anyone but Creed Harker in the stall. The gun contained only Harker's fingerprints. The medical examiner did the autopsy early this morning, and he reports that Harker's wound was consistent with a self-inflicted gunshot."

"Well, that's it," the captain said, "in the absence of any other evidence."

Morris removed a plastic evidence bag containing a handkerchief from his pocket. "We did come up with one thing that I haven't been able to explain. We searched the various trash cans in the lobby, which was routine, and just outside the front door we found a man's handkerchief, neatly folded."

"Anything odd about it?"

"It's made of a very fine linen and appears to have some age on it. It had been starched and ironed and it had oily stains that might be gun oil, as if it had been used to wipe a gun clean of fingerprints. It bears no manufacturer's label and no laundry marks, indicating to me that it was custom-made and had only been laundered and ironed in the home."

"Well, shit," the captain said, "I was hoping that we could announce to the press that this case is closed. No indication of who it might have belonged to?"

"There was an elderly man sitting near the men's room, who left the hotel by that entrance. He might have thrown it away as he left the hotel."

"Who was he?"

Morris read from his notebook. "A Mr.

289

Elton, apparently."

"Did anyone see this Mr. Elton deposit the handkerchief in the trash can?"

"There are no witnesses to that effect."

"So, it could have been deposited there by anyone leaving or arriving at the hotel at any time?"

"That's correct, sir."

"Well," the captain said, "in my book it's not evidence, since it has no identifying marks and no witness who can connect it with any person."

"I'm inclined to agree, Captain," Morris said. "I just thought I ought to mention it."

"What about the gun Harker used? Was it registered to him?"

"No, sir, the serial number tells us it was sold to the U.S. Army in 1949. It's a .45 Colt, of a size that makes it issued to general officers. Army records are not computerized back that far, and I have no reason to think that a paper trail exists. However, Harker's secretary told us that he collected weapons of various kinds, and it could very well have been part of his collection."

"Okay, we've pursued this case to its natural conclusion," the captain said. "Death was by self-inflicted gunshot wound, using the man's own gun. I'll announce it to the press at my noon media conference.

Any objections from anybody?"

Nobody spoke.

## 52

Stone sat at his desk and looked at his wristwatch. It was mid-morning, and Mary Ann Bianchi had not phoned. She was the first step in setting up everything, and he itched to call her to find out what was going on. Before he could do that, his attention was drawn to a bound document on his desk, titled *Journal, Volume I,* which lay on the first of Eduardo's red leather-bound, handwritten volumes. That was fast, he thought. Anna Fontana had been working for only two days in the office next door.

Stone flipped open the binder. The first entry was dated January 1939.

I met, at his request, with M.L. in an apartment on Broome Street, downtown. The place was nicely furnished, but it did not appear to be lived in, just used for meetings. I had just arrived when C.L. joined us, in the company of two men who appeared to be bodyguards.

M.L. immediately asked me my age; when I told him I was nineteen, he at first seemed shocked, then intrigued. He began asking me questions about myself, to which I gave only terse answers. C.L. looked at me in disbelief and seemed ready to dismiss me, until I pointed out that I had been invited there. I had had no previous business relationship with either of these men, nor anyone who knew them, to my knowledge. I did not know who had introduced us.

M.L. took a new tack, asking my advice about the price of genuine scotch whiskey. I told him I could supply him with twenty cases immediately and named a price. C.L. laughed and said that was less than the wholesale price. I told him I would be happy to sell it to him at the wholesale price. M.L. thought this amusing and pointed out to C.L. that Prohibition was long gone, and scotch was plentiful at the wholesale price. He asked me if I could supply more than twenty cases, and I replied that I could, but not immediately; it might take another week or two. M.L. accepted my price and asked where he could collect the shipment. I told him that I would require payment of the entire sum in advance and that I would deliver it to any local address he wished within twenty-four hours.

C.L. objected to this arrangement and asked me why they should trust me. I told him that whoever had recommended me to them must have thought me trustworthy, and since I was clearly the weaker hand in the transaction, I would need advance payment to protect my position and to be of further use to them. I said that if this was not satisfactory to all concerned, we could forget the whole business and that I would sell my scotch elsewhere. I thanked them for their time and made to leave.

M.L. stopped me. He opened a briefcase and counted out the sum in large notes. I asked him if he would like a receipt, but he said that my beating heart was his receipt and that if I did not deliver on time it would be removed and delivered to him. I agreed to this arrangement, and he instructed me to deliver the whiskey to the basement of the building we were in. Suffice it to say, I was motivated to make the delivery on time, and M.L. and I agreed to do further business on the same terms.

Stone thought that M.L. and C.L. might well be Meyer Lansky and Charlie Luciano, and that Eduardo must have been selling them stolen scotch whiskey.

Then Joan buzzed him and said Mary Ann was on the line. Stone pressed the button. "Good morning, Mary Ann," he said. "Where are we in all this?"

"I told Dolce that you needed to meet with the two of us about some business with the estate."

"And . . . ?"

"She agreed to have us for lunch at Papa's house Monday at one PM."

"I should think that's enough time to make the necessary arrangements."

"She wanted to meet today, but I thought Dino would need more time than that. I mean, this is all very complicated."

"Yes, it is certainly that. I'd better get to work on my end right now."

"Can I ride out there with you on Monday?"

"Of course. I'll have Fred pick you up at eleven forty-five."

"At my office, please."

"As you wish."

"Stone, I'm frightened."

"I understand your concern," Stone replied, "but I think this will be our only opportunity to bring this off without public notice."

"I suppose this will be expensive."

"Breathtakingly so. I can't tell you how much now, but brace yourself."

"All right, I'm braced," Mary Ann said. "I'll see you on Monday."

Stone hung up and called Dino. "Mary Ann and I are going to lunch at Eduardo's house on Monday at one. Is that going to work for you?"

"I can make it work," Dino said.

"I'm concerned about Pietro."

"And well you should be." Someone interrupted Dino. "I'll call you when everything is set and run you through it."

Stone called Mike Freeman and told him what he needed.

"I can do that," Mike said.

"And no freebies, Mike. Bill this to me, and I'll see that it's paid in full immediately. No discounts, either."

"As you wish, Stone."

Stone hung up, satisfied that all the bases would be covered, but still, he was filled with dread. He did not wish to be in the same room with Dolce, not even with Mary Ann there, but now he was committed, and he would have to go through with it. And he would have all weekend to worry about it.

## 53

Elton Hills had an early lunch in his son's study and watched C-SPAN, which was featuring a live session of the House of Representatives. He watched as the House minority leader spoke against a bill sponsored by the other party. Elton knew that face from the newspapers he had begun reading, and he knew the man's voice from the tape Bruce Willard had played him of the meeting that Evan had attended and, later, exposed. The voice grated on his nerves.

Elton looked up the number of the House in the phone book and, when it was answered, asked for the office of Representative Evan Hills.

"Good morning," he said to the young man who answered. "My name is Elton Hills. I am the father of Congressman Hills, and I wonder if I might speak to his chief of staff?"

"Just a moment, Mr. Hills."

He was kept on hold for about a minute, then a young woman came on the line. "Mr. Hills?"

"Yes."

"This is Elaine Tozer. I'm Congressman Hills's chief of staff. May I express the sincere condolences of all of us in his office on your terrible loss?"

"Thank you, Miss Tozer," Elton said. "That is very kind of you."

"Not at all. Is there something I can do for you?"

"Actually, there is. I wonder if I could come to the Capitol and see my son's office? I'd like to know where he worked."

"Of course you may, Mr. Hills. I'd be delighted to receive you here and take you to his office."

"Is there a room number?"

She gave it to him. "How will you be arriving?"

"In my car, with a driver."

She told him how to get to the garage and said she would arrange a visitor's parking pass. "I'll be happy to meet you in the garage and bring you to Evan's office. When would you like to come?"

"Would an hour from now be all right?"

"Of course. I'll meet you in the garage at

that time."

Elton thanked her, then he packed his things, left the housekeepers a note and a hundred-dollar bill, and went to his waiting car.

Elaine Tozer was a small, trim woman in her forties, dressed in a business suit. She greeted him warmly and led him to the elevator. Once aboard, she clipped a plastic tag to his coat pocket that read: VIP GUEST. "That will get you through security and anywhere you want to go in the building," she said.

She kept up a running chatter as they got off the elevator and walked to Evan's office. She took him into the handsome room. "I'm so glad you could come today," she said. "Tomorrow we have to dismantle the office and prepare it for an appointed successor, who will serve out Evan's term."

"Do you think I could spend some time here alone?" Elton asked.

"Of course. We won't be needing the room this afternoon. Would you like some coffee or tea?"

"No, thank you. I'd just like to sit here quietly and commune with the spirit of my son."

"I'll leave you alone, then." She left the room.

Elton had a look around the office and found it much like his son's study. There were no photographs of him with politicians or celebrities as he might have expected to find in a politician's office. He sat down at the desk and idly opened a drawer or two, and in the right-hand top drawer he found something he had not seen for a long time: it was the small 9mm semiautomatic Walther pistol that his elder son had bought somewhere. It had apparently been the World War II sidearm of some German officer. The elder boy must have given it to Evan, he thought.

As he held the gun, a television set across the room came to life, apparently on a timer. The channel was C-SPAN, and the camera was directed at the floor of the House of Representatives, where a man stood at a podium, speaking. He recognized the Speaker from his pictures in the newspaper. A thought came to him. He went to the door leading to the reception area and locked it, then returned to the desk.

He found a book about the Capitol building, and inside it, a plan of the House wing. He noted that Evan's office was quite near the House floor. The route from one to the other was simple.

Elton field-stripped the weapon, and

cleaned it, as he had the .45, then he wrapped it in a handkerchief and slipped it into his coat pocket, thinking hard. He glanced back at the TV set; the House was adjourning. It was a wild chance, but as long as he was in the building and armed, why not?

Elton found a roll of tape in his son's desk and walked to the rear door of the office, which opened into a hallway. He opened the door, pressed back the spring-loaded bolt, and taped it into place. He looked both ways up and down the hall, then let himself out and pulled the door closed behind him. He reckoned he had a walk of less than a minute. His VIP GUEST pass got him deference from everyone who might have questioned his presence. After all, he was an ordinary-looking elderly man in a tailor-made suit — not the sort to attract interest.

As he reached the House chamber the doors opened and people began to stream into the hallway, the session having ended. He stood by the door and looked inside; he saw the minority leader standing in the aisle, talking with some people, then the man left the others and walked toward the main doors.

"Excuse me, Mr. Speaker," Elton said to him.

The man's eyes went to the pass, then to his visitor's face. "Yes? Can I help you, sir?"

"I am Elton Hills, the father of Congressman Evan Hills." He watched the man's expression change from solicitous to stone cold. "I have no time for you," he said.

"I have a message for you from my son. He asked me to deliver it in person. Is there somewhere we could be alone for a moment?"

The man looked annoyed. "This way," he said, leading Elton through the doors and making a turn. They appeared to be in the House cloakroom. The man led him to a curtained alcove and pulled the velvet drapes shut. "Now," he said, "what is it?"

Elton gave him a little push that caused him to fall into a chair.

"Now, see here, Mr. Hills."

Then Elton had the gun in the man's mouth. "This is my son's message," he said, and pulled the trigger. The pistol was not as noisy as the .45 had been. Elton quickly wiped the weapon and saw that the man's fingerprints and blood were put on it, then he turned and walked back to the main doors and left with the last of the congressmen leaving the session.

Elton dropped the handkerchief into the first wastebasket he saw, then he walked back to his son's office, not hurrying, and, after ascertaining that no one was watching, entered through the taped door. He stripped off the tape and closed it behind him, then he unlocked the front door of the office and went and sat at his son's desk. He could hear alarms going off somewhere. He went into his son's private powder room, washed his hands thoroughly and made sure there was no trace of blood on him, then he went back to the desk, picked up the phone, and dialed Bruce Willard's cell number.

"Hello?"

"Bruce, it's Elton. I'm back home in Pennsylvania, and I just wanted to thank you again for your kindness to me last evening."

"Elton, have you heard what happened at the hotel while we were there?"

"No, what happened?"

"A man named Creed Harker shot himself in the men's room, about the time you were there."

"The name doesn't ring a bell," Elton said.

"Is there anything you need to tell me?" Bruce asked.

"No, I don't think so. I just wanted to thank you again. Oh, here comes my lunch. I'll talk to you soon." He hung up and sat down at his son's desk. He was still sitting there when Miss Tozer returned to the office.

"I'm sorry to have left you alone for so long, but we had an incident in the members' cloakroom that's had us pretty busy for the past hour."

"Not at all. I've enjoyed soaking up the atmosphere here," Elton replied.

"The halls are clear now. May I walk you back to the garage?"

"Thank you, yes." They returned to where Manolo sat in the Bentley, waiting. He gave her back the badge. "Thank you so much for your kindness, Miss Tozer," Elton said.

"I'm so happy to have been able to meet you," she replied, shaking his hand. "Your son was a wonderful man."

"I know," he said. Manolo opened the door, and he got into the rear seat. "Let's go home," he said, and relaxed into his seat.

His last thought before he dozed off was that, perhaps, he should have strolled over to the Senate and shot Henry Carson, too.

As he got out of the car in his driveway at home, he spoke for a moment with Manolo. "If anyone should ask, we got home about three hours ago," he said.

"As you wish, Mr. Hills," Manolo replied.

# 54

Late in the afternoon, Stone stepped into the office where Anna Fontana was working. "I read the first volume with great interest," he said. "Thank you."

"You're very welcome. It's going quite well, I think."

"I think I mentioned that Carla is coming up for the weekend."

"Yes, you did. I'm seeing her for lunch tomorrow."

"Well, she just called from a cab, and she should be here in half an hour or so. Would you like to have a drink with us before you go back to Brooklyn?"

"Why, yes, that's very kind of you."

"If you're finished for the day, I'll walk you upstairs to my study."

She gave him her work papers for the day, and he locked them in his safe, then went upstairs with Anna, settled her on the sofa in his study, where she asked for a martini.

"Runs in the family, I guess," Stone said, pouring one and handing it to her.

"Quite a lot runs in the family," she said. "More than you know."

Stone poured himself a Knob Creek on the rocks and took a chair opposite her. "Oh?"

"I've had a peek forward in the journals," she said, "and I'm afraid they will cover a period when Eduardo's life and mine overlapped."

"Afraid?"

"It's a subject that I've been avoiding for many years."

"How did you meet?"

"In an Italian grocery store downtown," she replied. "I went there once a week to stock up on sausages, cheese, and other things the supermarkets didn't carry. We had both been offered a taste of some bresaola in the aisle, and we compared notes. He was charming, well-spoken, and beautifully dressed. I suppose it helped that he was older than I, since I had always been attracted to older men."

"And what came of this meeting?" Stone asked.

"Carla," she said.

That stopped Stone in his tracks. He couldn't think of anything to say.

"I was married, of course, and we had a perfunctory sex life, but it was quite something else with Eduardo."

"So, Carla's father could have been either of the two men?"

"It seemed so. I told Eduardo of my dilemma and asked his advice. I had been considering an abortion, which, at that time, was illegal but available if you knew someone. He talked me out of the abortion and said that he would be quite happy to have another child, if I would, and that he would take on a father's responsibilities. My husband and I had been childless up until then, and I had wanted a child, but he had not. I went home and told him I wanted a divorce. He moved out the next morning, and he agreed to a Mexican divorce, since it would save him a lot of money on legal fees. When Carla was born, Eduardo was there, and when he saw her he knew Carla was his, no doubt, and from that moment on, he saw that we had a comfortable life and that Carla was well educated."

"Did you tell her?"

"No, I never have. She met him, perhaps a dozen times. After his wife died he proposed to me, but I thought it was too late for such an upheaval in both Carla's life and mine. But the dilemma is back. Now you know, and depending on what use you make of the journals, a great many other people could soon know."

"I suppose that's a possibility. In that unlikely event, I'll take steps to be discreet."

"I'm going to tell her as soon as she arrives," Anna said, "and I'd appreciate it if you would be with us when I do."

"If that's what you wish." The doorbell rang, and Fred went to get it. A moment later, Carla walked in.

"What a surprise," she said, kissing her mother. "Did you change your mind about dinner?"

"No, I just stayed for a drink, and I have something to tell you, so get a drink and sit down."

Stone made them all a drink, then sat down and shut up.

Anna began to tell the story again, while Carla listened, transfixed. When her mother had finished, Carla took a swig of her martini and set it down. "I knew it," she said.

"How could you have known?"

"Because Eduardo was the only father I ever had. I met your husband only a couple of times."

"Well, he moved to the West Coast."

"Those times when we visited Eduardo

were like going home to my father. I always thought of him that way. We saw quite a lot of him until I went to Yale."

"That's right, we did," Anna said. "Well, I'm glad you're happy with the knowledge."

"I'm perfectly happy with it," Carla said.

Anna looked at her watch. "Time for me to go. Dinner is uptown, near Columbia University."

"I'll have Fred drive you," Stone said, "and I won't take no for an answer."

They both said good night to her, and Fred took her down to the car.

"Wow," Carla said when she had gone. "I feel different somehow."

"I can see how you might."

"I want to read those journals when she's through translating them," she said.

"I think you have the right," Stone replied.

Still, he wanted to read them first.

# 55

Sergeant Avery Morris was at his desk in the homicide bureau of the DCPD when a television set in the corner of the room caught his eye — something about a shooting at the Capitol. A couple of other people moved to where they could see the TV better, and somebody turned up the volume.

Morris came over and watched long enough to hear that the minority leader of the House of Representatives had been found dead in the House chamber cloakroom with a handgun nearby. He whistled at his partner. "Jimmy, let's get out of here."

Jimmy Clark came over. "For this?" he asked, nodding toward the TV. "That's at the Capitol — not our jurisdiction. Let the Capitol Police and the FBI handle it."

"I'm just curious," Morris said. "You cover here, I'll be back in an hour or two." He went down to the garage and got into their unmarked car. At the Capitol he

310

flashed his badge to get into the garage, then took the elevator up a floor and walked to the office of the Capitol Police.

Morris had had occasion to visit the Capitol on business, and he had always made a point of treating the cops there as equals, not as security guards. He asked to see Howard Atkins, the chief, and was shown in immediately.

"Hello, Avery," Atkins said, standing up to receive him and pumping his hand. "Take a seat. Coffee?"

"Thanks, I will."

Atkins buzzed somebody and a uniformed cop came in with two paper cups on a tray.

"You hear our news?" Atkins asked.

"On TV. I came over because I have an interest. Can you describe the scene for me?"

"The minority leader ate his gun," Atkins said. "I haven't been able to draw any other conclusion. Of course, we're still talking to his family and staff. We hope to find something in his background that would explain this."

"I have a feeling you won't find anything that would explain it," Morris said.

"Tell me why."

"You hear about the guy in the men's room at the Four Seasons restaurant?"

"Yeah, sure. You think there's a connection?"

"Maybe. What kind of gun was involved?"

"An old Walther PPK, vintage World War Two."

"The one at the Four Seasons was a Colt .45, vintage Korea."

"So, two old guns?"

"Right, and I'll bet your Walther didn't have any prints on it or the cartridges except the minority leader's."

"Good guess, Avery," Atkins said.

"Tell me, Howard, did any of your people look at the trash cans in the area?"

"I'll find out." Atkins left the room for a moment, then came back. "My people didn't go into the trash. You want to do that with us?"

"If you don't mind, Howard."

The two men left the office together. "What are you looking for?" Atkins asked.

"I'll know it when I see it."

Two young cops did the work while the two older men watched. They found it in the third wastebasket. Morris pointed. "That's what I'm looking for." He put on some latex gloves. "If I'm right, it won't have any labels or laundry marks. Somebody washed and ironed it at home." He took the handkerchief from the young man and

312

unfolded it. "Identical to one I found in a wastebasket at the Four Seasons."

Somebody produced an evidence bag and put the handkerchief into it.

"So," Atkins said as they walked back to his office. "Is this somehow going to break our case?"

"I don't think so," Morris said. "What it tells us is that these two apparent suicides are connected. The two men did know each other. Creed Harker was a Republican lobbyist, I've seen his picture in the papers with the minority leader."

"That's very interesting," Atkins said.

"The two guns interest me, too. Harker was a collector, but I think when we look into it, the .45 won't be something from his collection."

"It sounds like what we need is a suspect with some more of those handkerchiefs in his dresser drawer."

"Or a gun collection with a couple of missing guns."

"Did your people find anyone of interest to talk to?"

"A couple of dozen people, but all credentialed for the House. We've got a tight security system here."

"I don't doubt it."

"Tell you what we're going to do, Avery,"

Atkins said. "We're going to start all over and question everybody near the scene again."

"I won't get in your way, but I'd like to hear what you find out."

"I'll call you tomorrow morning."

The two men shook hands, and Morris went back to the garage and got his car. All the way back to the station he racked his brain. Nothing new came to him.

# 56

Stone didn't sleep well, even after an athletic hour in bed with Carla. In the middle of the night, he put on a robe and slippers and went down to his office. He opened his big safe and took out the red leather notebooks of Eduardo's journal. It troubled him that he had to learn of Carla's relation to Eduardo from a coincidence involving his choice of a translator. He had thought he knew everything about Eduardo's estate, except for what money he might have hidden from the IRS.

He began leafing through the journal, which he couldn't read, looking for initials. In the fourth journal he found a reference to *A.F.* He pored over the Italian, trying to make sense of it. He could not, but in the next volume he began coming across the initial *C.* Then he turned a page and found a sealed envelope. He used a letter opener to get at the single page inside, then he unfolded it and switched on his desk lamp. It was a codicil to his will, handwritten and witnessed like the other codicils he had found in Eduardo's safe. Apparently, Eduardo had kept it separate from the others and had intended for Stone to find it, since he had given him the journals. The codicil left two million dollars to Anna and made Carla an equal heir to his estate, along with Mary Ann, Dolce, and Ben. Eduardo had done the right thing.

Stone felt hugely relieved, because it had worried him that Eduardo would have been so solicitous of Anna and Carla for decades, then ignored them at the end. It had been out of character, but now all was put right. Except that, at a moment when the estate had been fully settled, he would have to explain this to Mary Ann. And worse, to Dolce. He did not relish the task.

Back in bed, he finally slept soundly. When he awoke, Carla had gone; she had mentioned an early meeting at the *Times.*

Late Saturday morning Bruce Willard took a stroll down Pennsylvania Avenue, looking into the shop windows, exchanging an occasional greeting with a competitor. He thought about what Elton had done about the sale of his personal effects and how he would handle it when the time came. He was going to need more storage space than he now had, and it would have to be especially secure as well as temperature and humidity controlled. He could afford to acquire the space now, what with his inheritance from Evan. He was thinking about that when a gray car pulled up to the curb next to him, and a window went down.

"Good morning," the man said. "I'm Sergeant Avery Morris, DCPD. We met at the Four Seasons the other day."

"Oh, yes," Bruce said.

"Will you join me in the car for a moment, please? I have some more questions."

Bruce took a deep breath as he walked around the car and got in. He was going to have to be calm and helpful while telling the man nothing. He got into the car.

"I asked you the name of the elderly gentleman you were with, and you told me 'Elton.' Was that a first or a last name?"

"A first name. I'm sorry, that's just the way I think of him. His last name is Hills."

"Who is he?"

"An interesting question: he's the father of a friend of mine, now deceased. He's led a very reclusive life for at least thirty years, and I think our dinner was the first meal he's eaten outside his home for thirty or forty years. Beyond that, I don't know how to explain who he is. He apparently lives on inherited wealth. I met him because I attended his son's funeral."

"How did his son die?"

"In a traffic accident in New York."

A tiny light went on in Morris's head. "Hit-and-run?"

"Yes."

"Was his son a congressman named Hills?"

That was out of the bag, now; time to be forthcoming. "Yes, Evan Hills."

"What was your relationship with him?"

"We were friends and lovers."

"Was Elton Hills upset about his son's death?"

"Yes, of course. Mostly, I think, he regretted not having been in touch with his son for many years."

"Sounds like you've gotten to know him very well," Morris observed.

"Well, we share a mutual interest in American antiques. I'm a dealer, and I spent several days in his home after the funeral, cataloging his possessions."

"Were there any guns among his possessions?" Morris asked.

"No, none that I saw. Wait, there were a couple of old muskets and a pair of dueling

318

pistols, all eighteenth-century, nothing modern."

"Did Mr. Hills somehow connect Creed Harker with his son's death?"

"I don't think he knows who Creed Harker is, or was, and I can't see how he might make such a connection."

"Did you know Creed Harker?"

"I had seen him around the Four Seasons, where I often dine, but we didn't know each other."

"How about the minority leader of the House of Representatives?"

"The one who just died? What about him?"

"Did you or Mr. Hills know him or know of him? Perhaps through his son?"

Bruce shook his head. "I never met the gentleman. Elton wouldn't have met him, either: he and his son had not spoken for many years, and Mr. Hills doesn't own a TV or read newspapers."

"Do you know if Mr. Hills carries a handkerchief?"

"Doesn't everybody? I have no specific information that he does."

"Do you carry a handkerchief?"

"Yes."

"May I see the one you're carrying now?"

Bruce reached into a hip pocket and

handed him the folded handkerchief. It was of white cotton, with blue edging.

Morris inspected it. "Where did you buy this?"

"At Brooks Brothers."

"Do you wash and iron your own handkerchiefs?"

"No, they go to the laundry, along with my shirts. I must say, Sergeant, that all this is mystifying. What is it you are pursuing?"

"A murderer."

"Well, Elton Hills is not a murderer, and neither am I."

Morris handed him back the handkerchief.

"Where does Elton Hills live?"

"In Pennsylvania, near Philadelphia."

"Do you have his phone number?"

"Yes." Bruce produced his address book and read it out. "I should tell you that Elton doesn't answer his phone. You'll hear a beep, and you can leave a message, but I wouldn't expect a call back."

"Do you expect to hear from him soon?"

"I have no reason to."

"Then why were you and Mr. Hills dining together?"

"He called me and said he wanted to see his son's house in Georgetown. I showed him the house and took him to dinner."

"Was he staying at the Four Seasons?"

"No, he stayed at his son's house and went home the following morning."

"Do you know when he left town?"

"I had a call from him, thanking me for dinner, at around one PM yesterday. He said he was back at home."

"How long a drive would that be?"

"Two or three hours, depending on traffic."

"Does Mr. Hills drive?"

"No, I doubt if he has a current license. He has a servant who drove him to D.C."

"Well, I'm going to have to speak to Mr. Hills."

"Good luck with that," Bruce said. "Are we done, Sergeant?"

"Yes, Mr. Willard. I may call you again."

"I'm right across the street, about six doors down." Bruce gave him a card. "Are you interested in antiques?"

"Only in old weapons," Morris said.

The two men shook hands, Bruce got out, and Morris drove away. Bruce continued down the street, not looking back.

Avery Morris went back to his office and called Elton Hills's number. When he heard the beep, he said, "Mr. Hills, my name is Avery Morris. I'm a Washington, D.C., police officer. Will you please call me? It concerns the death of your son." He hung up.

Late in the afternoon, Morris's phone rang, and he picked it up. "Sergeant Morris."

"Sergeant, my name is Horace Pettigrew. I'm an attorney in Philadelphia, and I represent Mr. Elton Hills. Mr. Hills doesn't take phone calls from strangers, and he asked me to speak to you. You called about his son's death? How can we help you?"

Morris had half expected something like this. "Mr. Pettigrew, is Mr. Hills acquainted with a man named Creed Harker?"

"Sergeant, Mr. Hills isn't acquainted with anybody. He has been a recluse for close to forty years."

"How about the minority leader of the House of Representatives?"

"Sergeant, Mr. Hills's circle of acquaintances is limited to his domestic employees and two or three members of my law firm. Everybody he once knew is now either dead or doddering."

"He is acquainted with a man named Bruce Willard."

"Ah, yes, a friend of Mr. Hills's late son who is a dealer in antiques. He recently cataloged Mr. Hills's home furnishings for estate purposes. I think it's safe to say that, outside his household, Mr. Willard is the first person he has met in several decades."

"Do you know Mr. Willard?"

"I do not. The only reason I know his name is that Mr. Hills has appointed him as the agent for the sale of his belongings after his death. He has no heirs. Is there anything else?"

"I would like to come and visit with Mr. Hills," Morris said.

"I'm afraid that's impossible," Pettigrew replied. "Mr. Hills does not receive visitors, and as you may surmise from my call, he does not speak to strangers."

"This is in connection to a homicide investigation."

"Sergeant, I can assure you that Mr. Hills has no knowledge of any homicide. Now, if you will excuse me, I must go back to work."

"I might leave Mr. Hills another message."

"As you wish, but do not expect a response from either him or me." Pettigrew hung up.

Well, Morris thought, I tried.

# 57

Carla came back to Stone's house in time for dinner. She showered and changed, then they went to Patroon, where they were meeting Dino and Viv Bacchetti.

When they were settled at a table and had a drink in hand, Carla spoke up. "I've been at a meeting all day, listening to the tape of the Georgetown meeting of Henry Carson and his cohorts and hearing the report from Strategic Services on their voice analysis of the attendees."

"And what was the verdict?"

"They positively identified the voices of everyone who said anything audible at the meeting, by comparing them with recordings from congressional hearings and press conferences. *They are nailed!* There'll be three pages in tomorrow's paper, including a transcript of the meeting, and it will be on the *Times* wire tonight, to all the major newspapers in the country."

"That's great news, Carla," Stone said, "and great reporting."

Carla took a gulp of her martini. "Thank God for Evan Hills," she said. "All we had to do was confirm everything he said, and the tape was the final nail in the coffin."

"What do you expect the result of all this will be?" Viv asked.

"Great embarrassment for the Republicans in Congress, but I'm not sure how long that will last. The next election is two years away, so they'll have time to paper over the story. You watch: pretty soon they'll be calling it old news and playing the blame game every time they get a question about it."

"The minority leader apparently took it harder than just being embarrassed," Dino said.

"I can't figure that out," Carla replied. "He wasn't the type to blow his brains out over a thing like this — he was very good at brazening his way through any embarrassment."

"So you think it was a homicide?"

"That's what's so crazy about it," Carla said. "How could anybody get into the Capitol with a gun, then walk into the House cloakroom, shoot a congressman, walk away? It seems impossible."

"Somebody with the right credentials,"

Viv said. "Somebody who wouldn't get noticed. A staffer? Another congressman? A Democrat, perhaps."

She laughed. "Your guess is as good as mine. The Capitol Police and the FBI are all over it, and they haven't come up with a thing." Carla looked around. "Where is the ladies' room?"

Stone pointed the way, and she left the table.

"You all set for your meeting on Monday?" Dino asked.

"I believe so," Stone replied. "What about your end?"

"Well, it's a lot more complicated than what you have to do," Dino replied. "More dangerous, too."

"More dangerous than Dolce?"

"Well, maybe not, now that you mention it."

"I think you're both crazy," Viv said. "You, especially, Dino. If this goes wrong, you're going to be out of a job. They'll drum you out of the department."

"You could say that about half the decisions I make," Dino said. "It goes with the territory, and I'm okay with that. Besides, Mike Freeman would be glad to have another Bacchetti over at Strategic Services."

Carla came back, and they ordered dinner.

■ ■ ■ ■

Will and Kate Lee had a late supper in the White House family quarters after a reception in the East Room earlier in the evening.

Will brought the Sunday *New York Times* upstairs with him, and they went over the big story of the day while they waited for their dinner to be served.

"I wish this had happened before the election," Kate said. "We might have won a few more House seats on the back of this story."

"If this had come out before the election," Will said, "they would have found a way to blame *me* for it."

Kate laughed. "They're very good at that, aren't they?"

"I think they teach a course in blaming the president at that CPAC shindig. You'll see, it'll be your turn soon."

"Oh, I think I'll get a pretty good honeymoon — until after the baby is born, anyway."

"That may be true," Will said, "and it may not be."

"And then we'll get a week of baby pictures in the papers and magazines."

"The country does love a baby, doesn't it?"

"All the world loves a baby."

"It's a pity we can't auction the pictures," Will said. "We'd be set for life on the proceeds."

"Maybe we should sell the pictures to somebody who'll give a lot of money to a good cause."

"Such as?"

"I don't know, the National Organization for Women? Planned Parenthood?"

Will laughed. "I like it," he chuckled.

# 58

Early on Monday morning Dino sat at a table in a police vehicle made to look like an ordinary camper and went over a well-marked large-scale map of the area that included the Bianchi estate.

"Okay," Dino said to the Special Operations captain in charge of the unit, "tell me how you're going to approach the house."

"We've got a detail of a dozen men up this creek at a little marina," the captain said. "At half past one PM they'll come down the creek by boat and land at the estate's dock, which can't be seen from the house. They'll conceal themselves in the woods around the old stone barn and wait for my command over the radio."

"What about the front of the house?"

"We borrowed the Scali painting company van, which is large, and we'll send that up the driveway to the service drive that branches off. We'll unload four men near the kitchen door, and they'll go in with buckets of paint and their weapons concealed in drop cloths. Once inside, they're going to have to play it by ear."

"I want you to explain to your people that this man may seem old, but he's very dangerous, especially with a knife."

"They already understand that, boss."

"And I want every one of them to understand that nobody is to risk his own life to take this guy alive. Do I make myself clear?"

"If he's armed, shoot first and ask questions later, right?"

"That's one way to put it. Another way to put it is: we don't have enough on this guy to convict him, but we know that he's the one who cut up the priest and who got rid of Carmine Corretti's body, which we haven't found yet. I do *not* want him to walk."

"I read you, boss," the captain said.

"Where's the white van going to be?"

"Right where we are now. They'll respond to my radio call to go in."

"How many people?"

"Three, and they know what they're doing."

"I want at least one armed cop with them."

"I can do that."

"Dress him for the occasion."

"Right."

"Now, we've had a change of plan. We're not sending the van to New Jersey, it's going right here." Dino tapped the map. "We worked it with the Feds."

"That's much more convenient," the captain said.

"Have the people in the van been told that this is a twenty-four-hour job for them?"

"That's been made clear."

"They've got the paperwork they need?"

"We've double-checked that — it's all in order."

Dino went over a list in his notebook. "Okay, that's all I've got. I'm going to the office, and I want you on your cell phone with me for the whole operation. I want to know, step by step, how it's going."

"I'll be in touch the whole time," the captain said.

"And remember, there will be two civilians in the house, and I don't want them roughed up in the process or, worse, shot."

"I'm on top of that, boss."

Dino was having trouble leaving the RV. "I hope to hell that I haven't forgotten anything."

"Don't worry, boss, we'll get this done right."

"I'm counting on that," Dino said, "and I don't want any statements to the press coming out of your unit, and I don't want any leaks, either. We'll make this public at the right moment."

"We're a tight bunch, boss, nobody's going to leak."

Dino shook the captain's hand, left the RV, and got into his car. "Okay, let's go to the office," he said to the driver.

He had never in his life been more nervous.

# 59

Stone closed his briefcase and took a few deep breaths. He was perspiring lightly, and he dabbed at his face with a tissue from the holder on his desk. Joan came into his office.

"This came for you by messenger," she said, handing him a small wrapped package. "No return address."

Stone accepted the package, waited for her to leave, then unwrapped it, exposing a plastic box. He examined the contents, then closed it and put it into his briefcase.

Joan buzzed him. "Fred is outside with the car and Mary Ann Bianchi," she said. She peered into his face. "You don't look so good. Are you feeling all right?"

"I'm fine," Stone said. "Gotta run." He left through the office's outside door and got into the waiting Bentley.

"Good day," Mary Ann said. He thought she didn't look so good, either.

"And good day to you. Fred? You know where we're going?"

"I do, sir," Fred replied, and the car moved out smoothly.

"Why do you and I have to do this, Stone?" Mary Ann asked.

"Because there isn't anybody else."

"I suppose you're right. I just hate doing it."

"If we do it properly, we'll only have to do it once."

"Well, that's comforting. Why do I have to go all the way there?"

"Because you're the only person who can do what you have to do."

"You're right, I guess. I don't know why I need to be told that, but I do."

"It's going to be all right, Mary Ann."

"It'll never be all right," she said.

"In a week, it'll be better. In a month, it'll be better still. In six months, it'll be like it never happened, I promise you."

"Promises, promises," she muttered.

As they approached the house, Stone said, "Fred, I want you to remain in the car, and I don't want you to get out, no matter what happens. When I leave the house, I'll open the car door myself. Don't get out."

"I understand, sir," Fred replied.

The day had begun sunny, but now dark

clouds were massing to the north, and Stone could see lightning in them. They were due for a nor'easter, according to the forecast.

They pulled into the drive, and Stone said, "Please open the trunk, Fred." He got out and retrieved two umbrellas, then pressed the button that closed the trunk. "Ready?" he said to Mary Ann.

"No," she said, "but I'll put on the best face I can muster."

Pietro met them at the door, put their umbrellas in a stand next to the front door, and escorted them to the library. "Lunch will be in here," he said, indicating the table, already set. "Would you like anything to drink?"

"Scotch," Mary Ann said. "Rocks. Make it a double."

Stone looked at her, alarmed. "A glass of sherry," he said. "A chilled fino." Eduardo had always kept that. Pietro left the room.

Stone looked at his watch; Dino's men would be on the move by now. "Go easy on the booze, will you?" Stone said to Mary Ann. "I may need your help before this is done."

"Don't count on it," she said. "I can feel myself coming undone."

"Well, suck it up! We're in this now, and there's no help for it."

"What about Pietro?"

"That will be taken care of."

Pietro returned with two glasses on a silver tray. "Miss Bianchi will be down shortly," he said, then left again.

Mary Ann sank into an armchair and tugged at her scotch; Stone stood at the fireplace, warming his ass. Rain began to beat against the windows.

"A perfect day for it," Mary Ann said.

"A perfect day, if this were a bad movie."

"That's exactly what it is," she said. "I want it to end."

The main door opened, and Dolce swept into the room, wearing a tan cashmere dress and a necklace of emeralds. "Hello, hello," she said, and turned to Pietro, who had silently entered the room again. "I'll have a glass of champagne," she said, "and you can put the bottle on the table." She turned back to her guests. "And how is everyone today?"

Stone had never seen her bubbly before, and he wasn't sure what it meant. "I'm just fine," Stone said.

"Me, too," Mary Ann replied, managing a weak smile.

"Sweetie," Dolce said to her sister, "you don't look all that well. Are you ailing?"

"No, I just didn't sleep well last night, and

I'm tired."

"Guilty conscience?" Dolce asked, then laughed. She tossed off the champagne. "Let's sit down. Soup is on its way."

They all took seats at the table, and Stone put his briefcase next to his chair. Lobster bisque was served, laced with sherry; a good dish for a rainy day.

"Business now or later?" Stone asked.

"Oh, let's finish lunch first, Stone," Dolce said, "then we can hear what you have to say."

"As you wish. How's the painting going, Dolce?"

"Surprisingly well," she replied. "I'm working faster than I usually do."

They finished the soup, and Pietro reset the table, this time with large steak knives. Stone didn't like the look of them.

Next he brought plates containing slabs of prime rib, a heavier lunch than Stone thought he could handle, but he tried. The knives were razor sharp, and they sliced through the thick meat as though it were warm butter. Pietro brought a decanter and poured a stout red that couldn't be seen through. Everyone busied himself with eating; no one spoke until Mary Ann put down her knife. "I can't eat any more," she said.

Stone put down his knife, too, even though

half his beef remained. "That was deli-
cious," he said.

"I'll have Pietro wrap it up, so you can
take it home," Dolce said. "I notice your
driver is still in the car. Can we give him
some lunch in the kitchen?"

"He brought a sandwich," Stone lied.
"There's a radio program he likes to listen
to at this time of day."

"What program?"

"One of those British game shows on
Public Radio. Fred's a Brit."

"Oh, yes, he is, isn't he?"

Pietro took their plates, then came back
and asked if anyone would like dessert. "It's
zuppa inglese," he said.

Stone shook his head. "Just coffee, please."

Mary Ann asked for the same.

When coffee had come, Dolce put down
her cup and said, "Now to business. What
do you have for us, Stone?"

Stone set his briefcase on the table,
opened it, and took out the new codicil that
Eduardo had left. He left the case un-
latched. "I have some news," he said, "and I
hope you won't think it unpleasant. Mary
Ann, Dolce, you have a sister."

*"What?"* Mary Ann spat, sitting up straight.

"I know who you mean," Dolce said. "It's
that little girl who used to come to lunch

with her mother. What was her name?" She thought for a moment. "Carla!"

"That is correct," Stone said, amazed that she had figured it out so quickly.

"What are you two talking about?" Mary Ann demanded.

"Many years ago, after your mother died, Eduardo had an affair for some years with a woman named Anna de Carlo Fontana. Together, they made a child, Carla."

"You're out of your mind!" Mary Ann said.

"No, he isn't," Dolce said. "I think I figured it out at the time, but I didn't say anything. I kept waiting for Papa to say something, but he never did."

Stone was surprised; for some reason, he had expected Dolce to refuse to accept the news, but it was Mary Ann who was resisting it. He held up the paper in his hand. "This is written in Eduardo's own hand and properly witnessed." He read it aloud to them. "So you see, Carla will have the same inheritance as you two and Ben."

"You mean we have to give part of our inheritance to this girl?" Mary Ann asked, horrified.

"No, Eduardo's will explicitly said that all bequests would be made after taxes were paid, and that the residue would go to the foundation. This just means that the foundation will get a smaller residue, but it will still have more than sufficient funds to operate as Eduardo wished."

"Well, then," Dolce said, "all is well, isn't it?"

"Do we have to meet her?" Mary Ann asked.

"Only if you wish to."

"Is she some penniless waif who will now be rich?"

"No, she is the *New York Times*'s bureau chief in Washington — a very substantial person."

"I think it's funny," Dolce said.

Then there was a loud crash from the kitchen, and men were shouting.

Dolce reflexively picked up her steak knife, stood, and faced the door.

"Dolce, it's all right," Stone said.

"Shut up!" Dolce commanded, holding the knife in a defensive manner.

Oh, shit, Stone thought, it's now or never.

## 60

Stone reached into his briefcase, opened the small plastic box, and removed the syringe. He uncapped it, squirted out a little of the liquid to get rid of the air bubbles, and moved quickly toward Dolce, who still stood, facing the kitchen door, the knife out in front of her.

Stone reached around her shoulders and held her still. "Relax, Dolce, just relax." He stabbed the syringe into her upper thigh and emptied it into her. At the same moment, he felt a searing pain in his upper left arm. Dolce pulled away from him; Stone looked and found his left arm gushing blood down his sleeve and onto the floor. She had cut right through his suit.

"Holy mother of God!" Mary Ann shouted.

Dolce looked dazed and swayed on her feet.

Mary Ann ran to Stone, grabbed his

necktie, and in one motion, tore it off him. She wrapped it twice around his upper arm and pulled it tight. "Hold this in place," she said. "She's cut a major artery. If you don't keep the tourniquet tight, you'll bleed out in no time."

Stone kept the necktie tight. Dolce started for him with the knife, but she was unsteady on her feet. Then she stopped, her eyes wide, and fell forward like a tree onto her face.

"What was that?" Mary Ann asked.

"Thorazine," Stone replied. "The gift of a friend." He sat down heavily on a chair, dizzy.

Then Pietro burst into the room, a knife in his hand, and ran toward the hallway doors at a dead run, with two SWAT officers in hot pursuit. Stone heard the front door slam and looked out the windows toward the front lawn. Pietro disappeared into the heavy rainstorm, running like a deer, with the cops hard on his heels.

Mary Ann ran into the kitchen. "Dino!" she yelled at the top of her lungs.

An officer came to her. "The commissioner isn't here. What is it?" he asked.

"Mr. Barrington needs an ambulance right away — he's had an artery severed."

"We have a medical team on the way," the

342

man said, and he spoke into a handheld radio. "They'll be here in one minute."

"Tell them they're going to need two gurneys," Mary Ann said.

Stone was impressed with the way she had taken charge, saving his life into the bargain. "How'd you know about the artery?" he asked.

"I was a Girl Scout — we took a first-aid course."

Four people in hospital scrubs burst into the room, one of them pushing a gurney.

"Treat him first," Mary Ann said, pointing at Stone. "He's got a severed artery in his arm."

Two of them went to work on Stone, cutting off his sleeve and tending to the wound. "We've got to get him to a hospital," one of them said. "He'll need surgery to repair the artery." He turned back to Stone. "Do you know your blood type?"

"O positive," Stone said. The two men helped Stone onto a gurney.

Two more people appeared with another gurney and lifted Dolce, now semiconscious, onto it. They made a little procession toward the front door. When they opened it the rain was still pouring. They grabbed Stone's two umbrellas from the stand and sheltered the two gurneys as they got them both into a large ambulance. Mary Ann and an EMT got in with them, and the doors were closed.

"Let's get this guy to the hospital first," the man shouted at his driver.

"No!" Stone said. "Get to Floyd Bennett first. I'll be fine."

He didn't feel fine, but he wanted Dolce on her way.

"I guess it's okay," the nurse said. "It's on the way to the hospital, and he's stable." In minutes they were at Floyd Bennett Naval Air Station, a former base in Brooklyn that was little used these days. The Strategic Services G-650 waited on the tarmac with one engine running.

"How long is the flight?" Mary Ann asked.

"Nine or ten hours — it's a good forty-five hundred miles. The mother superior will meet you with an ambulance and her own medical team, and these guys will be with you all the way.

"Once there, you'll have a few words with the mother superior, so that she will have an official request from a family member of Dolce's, then you'll take off for Rome, where the aircraft will pick up some passengers for the trip back. That way, you only have to pay for the leg to Palermo."

"Thank God for that," she said.

The doors to the ambulance opened, and they made to remove Dolce and her gurney. But Dolce was hanging on to Stone's remaining coat sleeve.

"You!" she managed to say. "You!"

"Somebody had to do it, Dolce," Stone said. "You are a danger to yourself and others."

"You!" she said again, then the gurney was out of the ambulance. Mary Ann ran alongside it toward the big jet. The rain had let up considerably, and there was no more thunder.

Stone sat up, braced on his good elbow, and watched through the open ambulance doors as the EMTs loaded Dolce's gurney onto the airplane. They already had her strapped down and an IV running as she disappeared into the aircraft. The door was closed, and the second engine began to spool up with a loud whine. In a moment the airplane was taxiing.

"Now you can get me to a hospital," Stone said, then he fainted.

He was out until the following morning, and sun was streaming through the windows of his room as his eyelids fluttered. A nurse sat by his bed, and Carla sat on the other side.

"Just take it easy," the nurse said. "You've

been sedated. The doctor will be here in a moment."

"Dino called me," Carla said, looking at her watch. "I've got to be at a meeting in my publisher's office in forty-five minutes. There are rumors that the executive editor is retiring, and I expect it's about that."

"You're going to get it," Stone said.

"There's stiff competition from Ed Rodgers, the editorial page editor."

"Nevertheless. You're going to get a Pulitzer *and* the job. You'd better get going, you don't want to be late for this one."

"I'll call you later," she said. She kissed him and fled.

A young man in scrubs and a white coat strode into the room. "Good morning. I see you're awake," he said cheerfully. "I'm Dr. Lefkowitz, your surgeon."

"How old are you?" Stone said.

Lefkowitz laughed. "I get that a lot. Older than you think. You were in surgery for a couple of hours. We repaired the artery and you took three units of blood. We kept you sedated through the night to keep you from moving around. You've had a tetanus shot and an IV antibiotic, too."

"When am I getting out of here?" Stone asked.

"We'll keep you another night, just to be

346

sure there's no further bleeding or infection. You should be out of here this time tomorrow. Move your arm as little as possible. I'll check on you again later today." He turned on his heel and strode out of the room.

"I need my phone," Stone said to the nurse. "It should be in my jacket pocket."

"You're going to need a new jacket," she said, going to the closet and finding the phone. "And a new shirt, too. And some pants. Everything was soaked with blood." She handed him the phone, and he pressed a speed dial button.

"Woodman & Weld," Joan said. "Stone Barrington's office."

"It's me," Stone said.

"Thank God. Fred told me they took you away in an ambulance, but he didn't know where, and I couldn't get ahold of Dino."

"In a hospital somewhere in darkest Brooklyn. I had an accident, but I'm fine. I'll be home tomorrow morning."

"Are you sure you're okay?"

"I'm just a little fuzzy around the edges," he said. "It's the drugs. I'm going to need a change of clothes — suit, shirt, tie, shoes, socks, and underwear." He handed the phone to the nurse. "Tell her where I am."

Dino burst into the room. "You're awake!"

he said. "I was here last night when you came out of surgery, but they said you'd be out for a while."

"More than awake, I'm alive," Stone said.

"Mary Ann called. They made it to Palermo okay."

"And Pietro?"

"Suicide by cop. Did us all a favor."

"Is Dolce safely in the convent?"

"Yes, the transfer went well."

"Do you think they can hang on to her for a while?" Stone asked.

"For the rest of her life, I hope."

"We can hope," Stone said.

# 61

Stone was home before lunch the following day. They got him into bed, and Joan fussed around. He insisted on dictating letters to Carla and her mother and signed the checks.

"That's it," Joan said.

"FedEx those," he said.

"Carla called a couple of times. They wouldn't put her through at the hospital." The phone rang, and Joan got it. "It's Carla."

Stone took the phone in his good hand. "Hi, there," he said, more cheerfully than he felt.

"They wouldn't let me talk to you at the hospital."

"I just got home."

"Are you all right?"

"Fine. They've told me to stay in bed for a week, then I have to start physical therapy."

"Take that seriously — it's important."

"That's what my doctor said."

"I didn't get the job," she said. "Rodgers did."

"I'm sorry. It's because you're only a mere slip of a girl."

"That must be it," she said, managing a laugh.

"We'll talk more about this later," he said, "but I have to get some rest now."

"Of course you do. Don't worry about me."

"Carla, your life is about to change in a big way," he said. "You'll be glad you didn't get the job."

"What are you talking about."

"For one thing, you won't have me on your hands. I've decided I can see only one woman in our nation's capital."

"Rats," she said. "And at a time like this."

"This time tomorrow, you won't know I'm alive," he said. "Really. Now goodbye." He hung up.

He woke up in time for dinner, which was broth. Dino and Viv came and spent an hour with him, then he had to go to sleep again.

"You're spending Thanksgiving with us," Dino said. "In a wheelchair, if necessary."

He had forgotten the upcoming holiday. "I won't need a wheelchair," he said.

On Thanksgiving, he needed the wheel-chair, and his arm was in a sling, bound firmly to his body, so he couldn't move it.

"You're spending Christmas with us, too," Viv said.

A nurse came every day and changed his bandages. When they took him off the painkillers, it hurt. His physical therapist was a plump, middle-aged woman in her fifties, who was without mercy. She forced him to move his arm, exercise it, lift little weights.

He was more himself at Christmas. They exchanged gifts and ate a lot. The sling was a thing of the past.

"So, what does the New Year hold for you?" Dino asked.

"Flight school for the new airplane," Stone replied.

"I forgot. When is the delivery?"

"When I finish flight school."

"Where?"

"Wichita."

Dino sucked his teeth. "Doesn't sound like much fun, especially in the dead of winter."

"What place is fun in the dead of winter?"

"Key West."

"You're right."

The next day, Ann called from Washington. "I'm sorry I haven't called much," she said.

"It's okay, I've been busy. I'll see you for New Year's, though."

"I'm afraid not."

"Kate's working you on New Year's Eve?"

"It's not that, Stone. I've been seeing somebody."

"Uh-oh."

"Exactly. I can't do the inaugural with you, either."

"Anybody I know?"

"Andy Cardiff. He's going to be our congressional liaison."

"Working for you?"

"Reporting directly to Kate. We couldn't see each other otherwise."

"I wish you every happiness."

"Same here for you. You're all better, aren't you?"

"All better."

"Bye-bye, then."

"Save me a dance at the Inaugural Ball."

"Sure." She hung up.

"Damn!" he said aloud. "And I burned my other bridge!"

# AUTHOR'S NOTE

I am happy to hear from readers, but you should know that if you write to me in care of my publisher, three to six months will pass before I receive your letter, and when it finally arrives it will be one among many, and I will not be able to reply.

However, if you have access to the Internet, you may visit my website at www.stuart woods.com, where there is a button for sending me e-mail. So far, I have been able to reply to all my e-mail, and I will continue to try to do so.

If you send me an e-mail and do not receive a reply, it is probably because you are among an alarming number of people who have entered their e-mail address incorrectly in their mail software. I have many of my replies returned as undeliverable.

Remember: e-mail, reply; snail mail, no reply.

When you e-mail, please do not send attachments, as I never open these. They can take twenty minutes to download, and they often contain viruses.

Please do not place me on your mailing lists for funny stories, prayers, political causes, charitable fund-raising, petitions, or sentimental claptrap. I get enough of that from people I already know. Generally speaking, when I get e-mail addressed to a large number of people, I immediately delete it without reading it.

Please do not send me your ideas for a book, as I have a policy of writing only what I myself invent. If you send me story ideas, I will immediately delete them without reading them. If you have a good idea for a book, write it yourself, but I will not be able to advise you on how to get it published. Buy a copy of *Writer's Market* at any bookstore; that will tell you how.

Anyone with a request concerning events or appearances may e-mail it to me or send it to: Publicity Department, Penguin Group (USA) Inc., 375 Hudson Street, New York, NY 10014.

Those ambitious folk who wish to buy film, dramatic, or television rights to my books should contact Matthew Snyder, Creative Artists Agency, 9830 Wilshire Boulevard, Beverly Hills, CA 98212-1825.

Those who wish to make offers for rights of a literary nature should contact Anne Sibbald, Janklow & Nesbit, 445 Park Avenue, New York, NY 10022. (Note: This is not an invitation for you to send her your manuscript or to solicit her to be your agent.)

If you want to know if I will be signing books in your city, please visit my website, www.stuartwoods.com, where the tour schedule will be published a month or so in advance. If you wish me to do a book signing in your locality, ask your favorite bookseller to contact his Penguin representative or the Penguin publicity department with the request.

If you find typographical or editorial errors in my book and feel an irresistible urge to tell someone, please write to Sara Minnich at Penguin's address above. Do not e-mail your discoveries to me, as I will already have learned about them from others.

A list of my published works appears on my website. All the novels are still in print in paperback and can be found at or ordered from any bookstore. If you wish to obtain hardcover copies of earlier novels or of the two nonfiction books, a good used-book store or one of the online bookstores can help you find them. Otherwise, you will have to go to a great many garage sales.

# ABOUT THE AUTHOR

**Stuart Woods** is the author of more than fifty novels, including the *New York Times*–bestselling Stone Barrington and Holly Barker series. He is a native of Georgia and began his writing career in the advertising industry. *Chiefs,* his debut in 1981, won the Edgar Award. An avid sailor and pilot, Woods lives in New York City, Florida, and Maine.

The employees of Thorndike Press hope you have enjoyed this Large Print book. All our Thorndike, Wheeler, and Kennebec Large Print titles are designed for easy reading, and all our books are made to last. Other Thorndike Press Large Print books are available at your library, through selected bookstores, or directly from us.

For information about titles, please call:
    (800) 223-1244

or visit our Web site at:
    http://gale.cengage.com/thorndike

To share your comments, please write:
    Publisher
    Thorndike Press
    10 Water St., Suite 310
    Waterville, ME 04901